Stone Barrington ⟨✓ P9-CNH-303 enemy intent on disturbing law and order in the latest action-packed thriller from the #1 *New York Times* bestselling author.

Upon returning from a dangerous coastal adventure, Stone Barrington is looking forward to some normalcy with the leading lady in his life. But when a grisly crime arrives on his doorstep, along with some suspicious new clients eager for his help, Stone realizes peace and quiet are no longer an option.

As it turns out, the mastermind behind the malfeasance rocking New York City and the nation's capital wields a heavy hand of influence. And when Stone is unable to re-cruit those closest to the case to his side, he is left with few leads and a handful of dead ends. But with the help of im-portant people in high places—and the expertise of alluring new friends—Stone is more than ready to rise to the occa-sion.

Praise for the Stone Barrington Novels

Choppy Water

"The action builds to a satisfying double climax"
—*Publishers Weekly*

Hit List

"Fast-moving easy reading in the familiar Woods style."
—*Booklist*

Treason

"The witty banter among Stone and friends and his fre-quent bedding of willing women keep the reader turning the pages . . ."
—*Publishers Weekly*

Stealth

"Smooth, easy-reading escapism in the trademark Woods style."
—*Booklist*

Contraband

"Woods balances the criminal doings with loads of light banter and tantalizing glimpses of great sex."
—*Publishers Weekly*

Wild Card

"Fans of Barrington and his entourage will enjoy another installment in a series where price is no object for the hero when it comes to solving crimes and satisfying his material needs."
—*Booklist*

A Delicate Touch

"Woods continues to deliver satisfying escapist fare, with the Bondian Barrington outmaneuvering his foes yet again, always with high-tech gadgetry at the ready and a beautiful woman at his side."
—*Booklist*

Desperate Measures

"Woods creates another action-packed thriller for his readers to devour, with plenty of interesting twists and turns that make for a nonstop, can't-catch-your-breath read."
—*Booklist*

Turbulence

"Inventive . . . [An] alluring world of wealth, power, and crime."
—*Publishers Weekly*

Shoot First

"Smooth . . . The principal pleasure lies in watching the suave, resourceful Stone maintain his good humor and high lifestyle throughout all his travails."
—*Publishers Weekly*

Unbound

"Stuart Woods is a no-nonsense, slam-bang storyteller."
—*Chicago Tribune*

Quick & Dirty

"Suspenseful . . . The excitement builds."
—*Publishers Weekly*

Indecent Exposure

"[An] irresistible, luxury-soaked soap opera."
—*Publishers Weekly*

Fast & Loose

"Another entertaining episode in [a] soap opera about the rich and famous."   —Associated Press

Below the Belt

"Compulsively readable . . . [An] easy-reading page-turner."
—*Booklist*

Sex, Lies & Serious Money

"Series fans will continue to enjoy this bird's-eye view of the high life."   —*Booklist*

Dishonorable Intentions

"Diverting."   —*Publishers Weekly*

Family Jewels

"Mr. Woods knows how to portray the beautiful people, their manners and mores, their fluid and sparkling conversation, their easy expectations and all the glitter that surrounds and defines them. A master of dialogue, action and atmosphere, [Woods] has added one more jewel of a thriller-mystery to his ever-growing collection."
—*Fort Myers Florida Weekly*

Scandalous Behavior

"Addictive . . . Pick [*Scandalous Behavior*] up at your peril. You can get hooked." —*Lincoln Journal-Star*

Foreign Affairs

"Purrs like a well-tuned dream machine . . . Mr. Woods knows how to set up scenes and link them to keep the action, emotion, and information moving. He presents the places he takes us to vividly and convincingly . . . Enjoy this slick thriller by a thoroughly satisfying professional." —*Florida Weekly*

Hot Pursuit

"Fans will enjoy the vicarious luxury ride as usual." —*Publishers Weekly*

Insatiable Appetites

"Multiple exciting storylines . . . Readers of the series will enjoy the return of the dangerous Dolce." —*Booklist*

Paris Match

"Plenty of fast-paced action and deluxe experiences that keep the pages turning. Woods is masterful with his use of dialogue and creates natural and vivid scenes for his readers to enjoy." —*Myrtle Beach Sun-News*

Cut and Thrust

"This installment goes down as smoothly as a glass of Knob Creek." —*Publishers Weekly*

Carnal Curiosity

"Stone Barrington shows he's one of the smoothest operators around . . . Entertaining." —*Publishers Weekly*

Standup Guy

"Stuart Woods still owns an imagination that simply won't quit . . . This is yet another edge-of-your-seat adventure."
—*Suspense Magazine*

Doing Hard Time

"Longtime Woods fans who have seen Teddy [Fay] evolve from a villain to something of a lovable antihero will enjoy watching the former enemies work together in this exciting yarn. Is this the beginning of a beautiful partnership? Let's hope so."
—*Booklist*

Unintended Consequences

"Since 1981, readers have not been able to get their fill of Stuart Woods's *New York Times* best-selling novels of suspense."
—*Orlando Sentinel*

Collateral Damage

"High-octane . . . Woods's blend of exciting action, sophisticated gadgetry, and last-minute heroics doesn't disappoint."
—*Publishers Weekly*

Severe Clear

"Stuart Woods has proven time and time again that he's a master of suspense who keeps his readers frantically turning the pages."
—*Bookreporter.com*

BOOKS BY STUART WOODS

FICTION

Jackpot*

Double Jeopardy*

Hush-Hush*

Shakeup*

Choppy Water*

Hit List*

Treason*

Stealth*

Contraband*

Wild Card*

A Delicate Touch*

Desperate Measures*

Turbulence*

Shoot First*

Unbound*

Quick & Dirty*

Indecent Exposure*

Fast & Loose*

Below the Belt*

Sex, Lies & Serious Money*

Dishonorable Intentions*

Family Jewels*

Scandalous Behavior*

Foreign Affairs*

Naked Greed*

Hot Pursuit*

Insatiable Appetites*

Paris Match*

Cut and Thrust*

Carnal Curiosity*

Standup Guy*

Doing Hard Time*

Unintended Consequences*

Collateral Damage*

Severe Clear*

Unnatural Acts*

D.C. Dead*

Son of Stone*

Bel-Air Dead*

Strategic Moves*

Santa Fe Edge†

Lucid Intervals*

Kisser*

Hothouse Orchid‡

Loitering with Intent*

Mounting Fears§

Hot Mahogany*

Santa Fe Dead†

Beverly Hills Dead

Shoot Him If He Runs*

Fresh Disasters*

Short Straw†

Dark Harbor*

Iron Orchid‡

SHAKEUP

STUART WOODS

G. P. PUTNAM'S SONS
New York

PUTNAM
— EST. 1838 —

G. P. PUTNAM'S SONS
Publishers Since 1838
An imprint of Penguin Random House LLC
penguinrandomhouse.com

The Library of Congress has catalogued the G. P. Putnam's Sons
hardcover edition as follows:

Names: Woods, Stuart, author.
Title: Shakeup / Stuart Woods.
Description: New York : G. P. Putnam's Sons, 2020. |
Series: A Stone Barrington novel
Identifiers: LCCN 2020036334 (print) | LCCN 2020036335 (ebook) |
ISBN 9780593188323 (hardcover) | ISBN 9780593188347 (ebook)
Subjects: LCSH: Barrington, Stone (Fictitious character)—Fiction. |
GSAFD: Suspense fiction. | Adventure fiction.
Classification: LCC PS3573.O642 S53 2020 (print) |
LCC PS3573.O642 (ebook) |
DDC 813/.54—dc23
LC record available at https://lccn.loc.gov/2020036334
LC ebook record available at https://lccn.loc.gov/2020036335
p.   cm.

First G. P. Putnam's Sons hardcover edition / October 2020
First G. P. Putnam's Sons premium edition / July 2021
G. P. Putnam's Sons premium edition ISBN: 9780593188330

Printed in the United States of America
1   3   5   7   9   10   8   6   4   2

SHAKEUP

1

Stone Barrington stood under the portico of the Hay-Adams Hotel, in Washington, D.C., and shivered. It was January 20, and he was dressed in a dark blue pinstripe suit, a double-breasted cashmere overcoat, a black cashmere scarf, and a soft, dark blue fedora. His hands were crammed into soft black leather gloves with a cashmere lining, yet, after only three minutes of this, he was already freezing. A thermometer across the street read 22 degrees Fahrenheit.

A black SUV with darkened windows drove under the portico, and the doorman conversed briefly with the driver, then beckoned Stone. Another doorman opened the nearest door for him, and he slid into the warm interior.

"Mr. Barrington?" the driver asked.

"That's me."

"May I see your White House badge, please?"

Stone dug his way past the scarf and felt for the plastic badge on the silk tape that hung around his neck, then held it up so the driver could compare the face on the badge with the man holding it.

"Thank you, sir. Normally, it's a very short drive, but it may take us a little longer today. Lots of traffic."

It took twelve minutes before someone opened the rear door and Stone hurried through the next portico. His outer garments and hat were taken from him, and he was escorted to an elevator, which disgorged him onto the upstairs floor. A Secret Service agent opened the door to the family quarters and allowed him to enter. He knew the way.

He found the president of the United States, the former president of the United States, and the next president of the United States sitting before the fireplace, sipping from teacups.

"Come in, Stone, and have tea," Katharine Rule Lee said. "It's the custom, on Inauguration Day, for the outgoing president to have the incoming president for tea, prior to the ceremony."

Stone shook Will Lee's hand and kissed Holly Barker on the cheek, then asked for Earl Grey, with lemon. The president poured.

"I understand it's a bit chilly outside," Will said.

"I recommend outer clothing made to Antarctic standards," Stone replied.

"Typical," Will replied, "on Inauguration Day. How's the crowd?"

"I've only seen an aerial view on television," Stone said, "but the ground under the crowd was not visible."

"Oh, good. The networks delight in comparing the crowd size to the last president's."

Stone was only halfway thawed before they were summoned to depart. In the reception hall downstairs, his outer clothing was returned to him, and he was helped into it. Taking the jump seat beside Will in the presidential limousine, Stone marveled at the foot-thick doors, the three-inch-thick window glass, and the absolute silence inside. As soon as the women's garments could be arranged in the rear seat, they were off.

"The Bacchettis will be seated with us," Kate said. "I'm told we'll have electric blankets for our laps."

The Bacchettis were Stone's closest friends, he the police commissioner of New York City and she the COO of Strategic Services, the world's second-largest security company. Stone and Dino had been partners as detectives on the NYPD, when everybody was younger.

Only Kate and Will managed to make conversation: Holly was as silent as a rock, and Stone followed her lead. Holly slowly leafed through a document, her speech, in a leather-bound folder, her lips moving a little.

Amazingly, given the temperature, the streets on the way to the Capitol were lined with the public, six-deep. They were there to see the first female president succeeded by the second such. Crowd noise could be heard dimly through the thick glass, and Holly remembered to smile and wave. Stone sat perfectly still, as no one had come out in the freezing cold to see him.

As they dismounted from the tanklike vehicle, a band somewhere nearby began to play "Hail to the Chief" at the sight of Kate. They were led up some stairs to a row of seats behind the podium, where the Bacchettis awaited, along with the promised warm blankets. The crowd size lived up to the aerial photographs.

A clergyman intoned a prayer that was more like a speech, then the chief justice of the Supreme Court, a small woman, took the podium and held out a beckoning hand to the president-elect. Holly, dressed in a green suit that set off her red hair, took the oath, then addressed the crowd.

Stone didn't bother to listen, since he had read every draft of the speech during the past month. Instead, he searched the crowd in front of him, since he couldn't turn and look at those behind him. He spotted only one familiar face, and before he could remember the name, the speech ended, and Holly was given a very appropriate standing ovation. Then they slowly followed her back to the car, as she shook every hand along the path.

Holly was late to the White House luncheon given to honor her, because she wanted to sign a dozen executive orders and her appointment letters to her cabinet. She may have been, she said, the first president to have named them all before the inauguration.

After lunch, back in the family quarters, Holly gave Stone his first real kiss of the day, and it was welcome.

"Now," she said. "I have to take a nap, if possible, and

then dress for the balls tonight. You should do the same, then come back here in the car provided."

"I shall do so," Stone said, kissing her again, then departed for the Hay-Adams. He had about four hours to get that done.

Stone inserted the key card into the lock on his suite's door, and let himself in. He hung his coat and hat in the closet by the door, then turned and walked from the vestibule into the living room of his suite. There, sprawled before him on the floor, lit by the sunlight streaming into the room, lay a female, fully dressed and, when he put his fingers to her throat, apparently dead.

"Good God, Stone!" a voice behind him said.

He turned and looked at Dino, who had spoken, and his wife.

"What have you done?" Viv asked.

"Don't point that thing at me!" Stone said, throwing up his hands in mock terror.

2

Viv walked over to the woman and felt for her pulse. "Nonresponsive," she said, "and she's cool to the touch."

Stone walked to the desk and picked up the telephone.

"Stop!!!" Dino yelled. "Don't touch that!"

"I was going to call 911."

"Do you want the place flooded with EMTs and cops, or do want this handled discreetly so you won't have to answer a lot of questions at each inaugural ball?"

"Your way," Stone said.

Dino looked up a number on his iPhone and called it. "This is Dino Bacchetti," he said. "Urgent." He tapped his foot impatiently while he waited. "Deb, Dino. Fine, you? Good. I'm at the scene of a high-profile apparent homicide that needs to be handled discreetly. At the Hay-Adams. In my suite, which Viv and I share with Stone Barrington. None of us. We returned from the inauguration to find her on the floor of our living room.

Unknown to any of us. Undetermined, pending the arrival of the ME." He gave her the suite number. "Send them up no more than two at a time, a minute or two apart. Have the gurney brought up on the service elevator; it's a few steps away. You don't have to, but it couldn't hurt. See you shortly." He hung up. "That was Deborah Myers, chief of the Washington, D.C., police department. She's coming herself with others. Viv, will you stand by the door and admit people with the proper IDs? No maids or other hotel employees. Stone, you come with me."

They went into Stone's bedroom and Dino closed the door. "Tell me what you didn't tell me when we walked in."

"Nothing," Stone replied.

"If there's anything else I should know, tell me now."

"I'd be happy to do that, Dino, if there were anything. This isn't my first homicide, remember?" They had worked more than a hundred together on the NYPD.

They heard the doorbell ring and went back into the living room. A woman in civvies was hugging Viv, while a police sergeant, about six feet five, built like a pro linebacker, and very handsome, stood there and looked around the room for threats.

Stone and Myers were introduced, and he was impressed.

"Okay," she said to Stone, conversationally, "tell me your story."

"I don't have a story, so I'll just give you the facts." He did so.

"Have you ever fucked her?" Myers asked.

"I'd have to see her naked, to tell you that."

"Don't be a smart-ass, Stone. Have you ever fucked her?"

"Not that I recall," he said.

"Have you ever so much as met her?"

"Not that I recall. It's been a long time since I've met a lot of people lying dead in hotel suites."

"Stone and I were partners two hundred years ago," Dino said. "We worked homicide."

Another knock at the door, and Viv admitted two men: an impossibly youthful man, carrying a satchel, and a middle-aged one wearing a ski parka over surgical scrubs.

"I assume the victim is the horizontal one," the man said.

Deb Myers smirked at him. "Dr. Steinberg, Dino Bacchetti, commissioner NYPD, his wife, Vivian, and Stone Barrington, who tripped over the body."

"Not quite," Stone said, shaking the man's hand.

Steinberg knelt beside the body, felt for a pulse at throat and wrist, listened to her chest, then held a small mirror under her nose, to see if it fogged. He produced an anal thermometer and did his work, then he produced a small recorder. "Victim is a white female, aged forty to fifty, expensively dressed with corresponding jewelry. She's unresponsive and presumed deceased. Preliminary cause of death, strangulation. Time of death between one PM and three PM."

Another knock at the door. This time it was two detectives, both thirtyish.

"Just in time, gentlemen," Steinberg said. "She's dead. Do your thing."

Forty minutes later, the detectives had questioned everybody and made way for a crime scene investigator, who worked the scene. "Preliminary observation," he said, "she entered the suite either by admission or with a key, walked across the living room and met the assailant, who strangled her to death. She probably knew him, since her blouse was pulled out of her skirt and a couple of buttons were undone."

He left, right behind the corpse, and so did everybody else, but Stone, the Bacchettis, Deb Myers, and Valentino, which was how Stone had come to think of the large policeman.

"Shall I wait outside the door, Chief?" Valentino asked her.

"No, Rocco, you'd just attract too much attention," Myers replied. "Just sit down over there, while these nice people buy me a drink." She collapsed on a sofa. "Scotch, please," she said to nobody in particular. "I'm officially off duty now, if anybody cares."

Stone dealt with booze for everybody, then sat down himself. "Man oh man," Myers said, taking a swig. "As if I didn't have enough to do today. Now I have to go home and dress for four balls."

"I'm going to four, too," Stone said, "but I'm only dressing for one."

"Lucky you."

"Question, Chief," Stone said. "Do *you* know the victim?"

She looked at him sharply. "How did you know that?"

"Something in the way you dealt with her. Dino taught me that."

"She's Patricia Clark, Pat. Her husband is Donald—Don—big business guy, who's about to be the new secretary of commerce."

"I hope you won't need to tell that to our new president before tomorrow morning. It might ruin her evening."

"Well, I'm going to have to tell the victim's husband, and he might want to tell the boss. I'll suggest he call in sick."

"Is he a suspect?" Stone asked.

"They were planning a divorce, just as soon as he was confirmed by the Senate. That is conveniently unnecessary, now."

"Oops."

"Does anybody here know Don Clark?" Deb asked. Heads were shaken.

"Then what was his wife doing in your hotel suite? Who has keys?"

"The three of us. Ah, one other," Stone said. "I think you can exclude her from your investigation, since I left her to come here, and she couldn't have gotten here first."

"Name?" Myers asked.

"For the present, unavailable," Stone said.

"Where were you, Stone, between one and three?"

"Having tea at the White House with the Lees, then at the inauguration."

She picked up her large handbag, rummaged through
it and came out with an envelope, which held a photograph. She handed it to him. "See anybody you know?"
She asked.

Stone looked at the photograph of Holly at the podium, delivering her address. Over her shoulder, he could
see himself. He held it up. "That's me."

"How about the two people right behind you?"

Stone looked at them. "I don't know them, so this is
just a guess: Donald and Patricia Clark?"

"Bingo."

"I was never introduced to them, and I didn't see
them at the luncheon for, among others, the new cabinet, at the White House."

"You expect me to believe that?" Deb asked.

"I expect you to, once you've run down the speech
and figured out the exact time this was taken."

"Okay, Stone. You're no longer a suspect. Still, there's
something you're not telling me."

Dino spoke. "You're right. The name he has refused
to speak is that of our new president. He's her date for
today and tonight."

"Oh," Deb said, and polished off her drink.

"Well, Deb," Stone said. "If you'll excuse me, I think
I'll have a nap. I'd be grateful if you'd try not to ruin the
president's evening."

"I'll see what I can do," Deb said, rising. In a moment, she was gone, followed closely by Valentino.

3

Stone, Viv, and Dino were driven to the White House, where they were put through the entry drill again, then taken up to the family quarters. They were seated in front of the fireplace while a butler took their drink orders.

Holly swept into the room as they took their first sip, and they were all on their feet.

"Oh, sit down," Holly said, taking a seat next to Stone. "It's just us."

"You'd better get used to it," Stone said. "It's going to happen every time you walk into a room, for the rest of your life."

"I hate it when you're right," she said, accepting delivery of her drink. "This one's going to have to last for the first half of the evening," she said, raising her glass. "I'm going to have to remain semi-sober, which is a fine point somewhere between being charming and being an embarrassment."

"Don't worry," Stone said. "You'll do fine."

Half an hour later the butler entered. "Excuse me, Madam President," he said. "Your car is ready."

———

There were four balls at which Holly had to make an appearance. The first was for moderate donors and lower-level campaign staff, at an enormous armory somewhere. Holly shook about five hundred hands, then a unit of the United States Marine Band started to play a waltz. Stone took Holly's hand and let her lead him to the floor, which everyone cleared, except photographers and cameramen with handheld TV cameras. They danced two numbers, then were whisked out of the building and on to ball number two, in a hotel ballroom, which was peopled by larger donors and campaign staff who were being retained to work at the White House.

Holly shook another five hundred hands. She and Stone waltzed once and boogied once, in a restrained manner, then worked their way out of the building. Stone could see flashes of light in his eyeballs, induced by the strobes of the pro photographers.

The third ball was in a grander hotel ballroom and their work was a carbon copy of the last stop. Finally, they were back in the car, and Stone was not surprised that the time was just past ten o'clock.

The fourth ballroom was much smaller, with much richer people and top White House staffers and cabinet members. It was held in the ballroom of a large, private house, and Holly shook hands on a line that stretched across the room, where the host and a woman who looked like his mother greeted them with big smiles and hugs.

"I'm so sorry Pat couldn't be here," the man said. "She's down with a horrible migraine."

"That's all right, Don," Holly said to her new secretary of commerce. "We understand perfectly."

More perfectly than she knew, Stone thought.

This time, they were seated in comfortable chairs in the paneled library, where people wandered past for a handshake and maybe a selfie. They were even given some very good food, to keep them going a little longer.

Stone's eyes were glazing over, now, but he hung on, with Holly as his example, until they were back in the car. Dino and Viv were being driven directly to the hotel, while Holly and Stone were driven back to the White House.

"You know you can't come upstairs, don't you?" Holly asked.

"Of course," he replied. "We play only in New York."

"I'm glad you're being so understanding," she said.

"There's something I have to tell you before you go up," he said.

"You mean about Pat Clark's death?"

"You already know?"

"Deborah Myers stopped by earlier this evening and

gave me a full briefing. I was amazed at the way Don stood up to the evening. It was too late to cancel, and he insisted on hosting."

"You stood up pretty well, yourself," Stone said.

"I didn't have a choice," she replied. "I tried to stay in the moment. Do you have anything new to tell me?"

"Chief Myers knows everything I know. She gave me the perp interrogation for a while, but the ME's report and the photograph of you, me, and the Clarks at the inauguration nailed it down, so I don't have anything to worry about."

"Deb would have nailed you, if she could."

"I asked her not to tell you until tomorrow, but that didn't work."

"It's best this way. I don't have to play dumb."

The car pulled up to the White House portico, and Stone began to get out with Holly.

"No," she said, stopping him with a kiss. "Not even to the door. We don't want that photograph taken."

"I guess I have some things to get used to, as well," he said. "Sleep tight. Call me tomorrow evening, when I'm back in New York."

"Will do."

After she got out, the car moved to the gate, then the rear door opened. "We have another car for you, Mr. Barrington," an agent said.

Of course you do, Stone thought, getting out. He couldn't be seen being driven around alone in the president's limo.

Dino and Viv were sitting in the living room, watching TV, brandies in hand.

"You didn't stay the night?" Dino asked.

"No, we've agreed that that will happen only outside Washington. We can't even seem to be sharing a bed in this town."

"Is New York out of bounds, too?"

"No, we reckon we can manage there."

"So, you're going to be living a sex-free life most of the time?" Viv asked.

"We've never denied each other the company of other people."

"It'll be interesting to see how that works out."

Stone sat down on the sofa, sipped his cognac, and watched himself waltz on television.

4

They landed at Teterboro, and Dino's official car dropped Stone off at home. As Stone was about to insert his key in the front-door lock, the door opened, and a man who looked familiar stood there, his right hand behind him.

"Oh, hello, Mr. Barrington. I'm Agent Jeffs."

"Hello, Agent Jeffs," Stone said. Jeffs holstered his weapon and shook Stone's hand. "I'm alone, so you can stand down."

"I'm afraid not, sir. Washington has listed your residence and the Carlyle Hotel as places frequently visited by the president, so we'll have one person on duty here at all times. Otherwise, whenever the president visits you here, we would have to perform a full-site security inspection, which might take a full day and would certainly be inconvenient for you."

It was damned inconvenient, Stone thought. "Glad to have you aboard, Jeffs."

"My first name is Jefferson," the man said. "I'd be pleased if you'd call me Jeff."

Stone blinked. "Of course," he managed to say.

Fred, Stone's factotum, got the luggage inside. Then Stone changed out of his suit and went down to his office, where he was greeted by his secretary, Joan Robertson.

"Oh!" she enthused. "You waltz so divinely!"

"If you keep that up," Stone said, "I'm going to have to shoot you." He went to his desk and started to go through the stack of mail and messages. "I assume you've made the acquaintance of Agent Jefferson Jeffs," he said. "But you can call him Jeff."

The phone on his desk rang, and Joan picked it up. "The Barrington practice at Woodman & Weld," she said, then handed the phone to Stone. "Dino for you."

Stone took the phone. "Didn't I just see you somewhere?"

"Yes, but I have news unavailable until now."

"Shoot."

"Deborah Myers called. Her department is trying to clear Donald Clark of anything to do with his wife's killing."

"Well, there goes the easy suspect. Who do they like for it now? Me again?"

"Her lover, possibly one of several."

"How did he get into our suite?"

"There are ways to deal with electronic locks, and he apparently used one of them."

"Who is he?"

"Unknown at this time. They got a phone tip from

somebody, a woman, saying that Pat was screwing around and deserved what she got."

"Call me when they make an arrest," Stone said.

"Dinner tonight?"

"Give me a rain check. I still haven't recovered from all the waltzing."

"I thought you had more stamina."

"Not for waltzing. That really takes it out of you."

"Bye." He hung up.

"Poor baby," Joan said. "All tuckered out?"

"Completely tucked."

"I'll leave you to your nap, then."

"Will you ask Helene to send me a ham sandwich and a beer upstairs? I'll nap better if I'm fed."

At the word *fed* Bob, Stone's yellow Labrador Retriever strolled into the room, his tail clearly saying, I'll have something, too.

"I'll take care of it," Joan said.

Stone scratched Bob behind the ears, then down his spine, his dog's favorite thing. The tail told him Bob was glad to see him.

Stone woke at half past six, and his first impulse was to head up to Elaine's, his favorite joint since he was on foot patrol in Germantown. Then he remembered that Elaine had died a few years back, and her restaurant had soon followed. He picked up the phone, glanced at his watch, and called Dino.

"What?" Dino said.

"I changed my mind. P.J. Clarke's, half an hour?"

"Done." Dino hung up.

Half an hour later, Stone strolled into Clarke's. Dino was already drinking Scotch. The bartender saw him coming and put a glass of ice on the bar, then filled it with Knob Creek bourbon. Stone nodded his thanks.

"So," Dino said, "what happened to your waltzing fatigue?"

"A nap cured it. Where's Viv?"

"On her way to Hong Kong. Business, as usual."

The headwaiter signaled from the door to the back room that he had found them a table, and they elbowed their way through the crowd at the bar and were seated.

"I got a call from a guy at DCPD that somebody saw Pat Clark with a man at the Hay-Adams."

"Did they get an ID?"

"No, just a description."

"Tell me."

"Tall—six-three—on the slim side, dark hair, big hands." He nodded toward the door where a tall, slim man with dark hair and big hands stood, staring at them. He started walking toward their table.

"Did you conjure him up?" Stone asked.

The man stopped, dug out a wallet, and flashed a badge. "Evening," he said. "Art Jacoby, DCPD."

5

ino looked him up and down. "Have a seat," he said.

Stone introduced himself. "How are you, Art?"

"Not so hot."

"I've never known a cop who didn't have a complaint. What's yours?"

"I've just been transferred."

"To where?"

"New York. From Washington. We have a liaison office here."

"I know about that," Dino said. "A guy named Smith holds that spot."

"Not anymore. He's already on a train home."

"How'd you get so lucky?" Dino asked.

"Bad lucky. This is my first time in New York, and I don't know how to live here."

"It's a lot like living anywhere else," Stone said. "You'll get used to it."

"How'd you find us at Clarke's?" Dino asked.

"I heard you could get a decent steak here, and I just wandered in."

"Your luck is improving," Dino said, handing him a menu.

They all ordered dinner and a second drink.

"So," Dino said, sipping his Scotch, "did you screw up, or did the guy you're replacing?"

"I guess I did, though I wouldn't have thought it was screwing up to have an opinion about a case."

"What case, and what opinion did you have?"

"The Clark homicide," Art replied. "It was my opinion that the husband did it."

"He had a pretty good alibi," Stone said. "He was standing right behind the president at the inauguration when his wife was killed. I know, because I was there, too."

"I shouldn't have said he did it," Jacoby said. "I should have said he had it done."

"That's a different ball game," Dino said. "Motive?"

"A divorce that turned sour and was going to cost him half of everything he has, and he has a lot."

"How much does he have?" Stone asked.

"Roughly half a billion, and half of that is a bad divorce."

"Unarguable," Stone replied. "Who disagreed with your conclusion?"

"Little Debby Myers," Jacoby said.

"Ah," Stone said. "We've met."

"I heard. She doesn't like you much, either. But that's

what she thinks of more than half the world. And she's always right, of course."

"Has she persuaded the president that she's right? That Clark is innocent?"

"That's what she's trying to do."

"Well, the president is an ex-cop," Stone said, "so she's no pushover. Do Myers and Clark have a personal connection?"

"Rumor has it that they've been in the sack together, off and on, for years."

"The plot thickens," Dino said. "How good a rumor?"

"There are three or four important people around D.C. who claim certain knowledge."

"Were they in bed with them?" Dino asked.

"Funny you should mention that," Jacoby said.

"How many of them?"

"At a time, you mean?"

"Yeah."

"Apparently, three is the magic number for both Clark and Little Debby."

"Male or female?"

"They both like girls and boys. I confess that, on a couple of occasions, I was in there."

"Gee, I'm glad I'm not on that case," Stone said. "Who's screwing whom is always tough, but with a third party involved, it gets a lot more complicated."

"Well," Jacoby said, "I'm out of it. I've said my piece and filed a report to that effect, which has probably already been shredded."

"Did you keep a copy?"

"I did."

"Hang on to it," Stone said. "We've had word of a suspect. Is there some reason his description matches yours?"

"Sure. Isn't everybody six-three and skinny?"

"Hardly anybody," Stone said.

They hashed this over until their steaks arrived.

"Art," Dino said, "have you got an alibi?"

"Yeah, I was home, watching the inauguration. I wasn't on until six."

"Swell alibi," Dino said. "Were you in bed with anybody at the time?"

"Fortunately, I was," Jacoby said.

"Anybody the world knows?"

"A girl who has been rumored to spend time in bed with Clark and Little Debby."

"Perfect," Stone said.

"She's not anxious to be questioned, especially by Little Debby."

"Does the chief have a reputation as an interrogator?"

"She was an assistant DA for fifteen years and, as such, she terrified everybody."

"I think your girl should retain an attorney," Stone said.

"Stone's a lawyer. He always says things like that," Dino interjected.

"I can't afford to start hiring lawyers," Jacoby said.

"You might give some thought to that for yourself," Stone said, "but not the same one that the girl hires."

"See what I mean?" Dino asked.

"Look at it this way," Stone said. "A good lawyer

might get the case tossed in a hurry, especially if your mutual alibis hold up. If he can do that, he's a bargain."

"I don't think she wants to talk to a lawyer any more than she wants to talk to Little Debby," Jacoby said.

"You're forgetting that you are her alibi," Stone said, "just as she is yours. It's in your mutual interests to eliminate you both as suspects as soon as possible."

"He's not thinking like a lawyer," Dino said to Stone. "He's thinking like a cop."

"And he can go right on thinking that way, until other cops lock him up. Then he's going to start looking for a lawyer, and the media will have already had their field day with you."

"All right, will you represent me?"

"I'm not licensed to practice in D.C.," Stone said, "except at the Supreme Court. But I'll find you somebody good."

"How soon?"

"First thing in the morning. All the lawyers I know are dining on steaks and fine wines right now. Where are you staying?"

Jacoby scribbled something on a notepad, ripped out the page, and handed it to Stone.

Stone gave him his own card. "I'll call you," he said. "Try to resist calling me."

6

Dino gave Stone a ride home. "What do you think of this guy Jacoby?" Dino asked.

"I'm not sure what to think of him or his story," Stone replied.

"I'll check him out from our end," Dino said.

"I also don't know what to think of a grown man who's never been to New York City before."

"Weird," Dino said.

They pulled to a stop in front of Stone's house. As he got out of the car, he saw his front door open an inch or so, then close.

"Something wrong?"

"Yes," Stone replied. "The Secret Service is camping out here."

"They suspect you of something?"

"No, they have instructions to maintain watches at the Carlyle and here, on the grounds that the president will be visiting often."

"And the bad news is that you can't get laid in your own house with them hanging around."

"That's it," Stone said. "G'night." He closed the car door, walked up the front steps and unlocked the door.

"Evening, Mr. Barrington," a man said.

"You're not Jeff."

"You're very observant. I'm Carmichael, night shift."

"Welcome aboard, Carmichael," Stone said. "Now listen up, because I'm going to give you some new marching orders."

"Sir?"

"You see that door over there?" he asked, pointing to his left.

"Yes, sir. It leads to the house next door."

"That is correct. If you open it, the first door on the right is to a small apartment, which is unoccupied. During the hours of five PM to nine AM, you and your fellow agents are confined to that apartment—that is to say, when I'm in the house. I sometimes entertain, and I don't want to have to explain who you are. Clear?"

"It is to me, sir. I'm not sure how clear my boss will think it is."

"If he finds it the slightest bit foggy, tell him to call me, but not during those hours, and I'll explain it to him in terms he will understand. Got it?"

"Yes, sir."

Stone pointed at the door. "Good night. Sleep well. There are books there, and a TV, to keep you entertained. If anything goes wrong, I'll hit the panic button on my alarm system." He watched Carmichael leave, then went upstairs in the elevator. He had just gotten into bed when his cell phone rang. The calling number was blocked. "Hello?"

"Hello yourself," the president of the United States said.

"It's nice to hear your voice. I've just banished your Secret Service agents to an apartment next door, during the hours of five PM to nine AM," Stone said.

"Those are the hours when you might be, ah, entertaining," she said.

"You never know."

"I understand completely, and I will convey your instructions to the head of my detail, Claire Dunne."

"Not Bill Wright?"

"Bill got kicked upstairs to assistant director of the Secret Service. After a decent interval, he might become director."

"Congratulate him for me, after a decent interval."

"I'll do that. Are you feeling a little . . . shall we say, itchy?"

"Most of the time, with you way down there and me way up here."

"Well, I may be able to get to New York next week. If I do, I'll come give you a good scratch."

"At last, something to live for!"

She laughed heartily. "Same here."

"Tell me," he said. "What do you think of Deborah Myers?"

"Little Debby? That's what they call her at her department."

"One and the same."

"I found her efficient, businesslike. She didn't waste my time, and I like that quality in people."

"Well, I have further to report on Little Debby."

"Oh, good! Tell me!"

Stone told her everything Jacoby had said.

"Wow, that's quite a story," she said, when he was through. "So, you're saying that my nominee for secretary of commerce may have hired somebody to do in his wife?"

"In light of what I just told you, it seems a possibility."

"Now I have to wonder if I should continue his confirmation process in the Senate."

"Seems logical to wonder that."

"It's more than that. Given what you've told me, it's mandatory, even if I think he's not guilty."

"Ah, politics," Stone said.

"I've always thought it easy to make decisions, but it gets harder when you're dealing with contradictory information."

"If what Jacoby is suggesting is true, Clark being cleared in the investigation isn't really so important, is it? Especially, when his girlfriend is conducting the investigation."

"You're quite right. Mr. Clark will remove himself from consideration and be back at his home in New York in time for dinner tomorrow night. I'll get him a lift in a helicopter; he'll like that."

"So what brings you to New York next week?" he asked, since the subject of Clark was now closed.

"I haven't decided yet, but I'll think of something."

"What sort of telephone are you talking on?"

"A burner. I had some at home. Nobody is listening in."

"I certainly hope not; especially when we're talking about scratching itches."

"Certainly not."

"Have you given any thought to how we're going to manage this assignation?"

"Well, I don't think it can happen at the Carlyle. Too many people involved."

"Perhaps you should be driven here in a plain-looking vehicle, and just drive into my garage."

"That sounds doable, if I can get into the vehicle without being noticed."

"Wear a disguise."

"What do you recommend?"

"How about a burka?"

She roared. "Wonderful. It will cover every inch of me, won't it?"

"I think that's the intention. Don't worry, I'll remove it for you."

"Now, that I will look forward to," she said. "It just occurred to me that I don't need to wear anything under a burka, do I?" She hung up, leaving Stone to imagine that.

7

Holly Barker was working in her private study, off the Oval Office, when her secretary buzzed.

"Yes?"

"Mr. Donald Clark is here to see you."

"Send him into the Oval in half a minute. And get word to the helicopter that they're cleared to land and to keep her engines running." She tidied her desk, then went into the Oval Office to be sure everything was tidy there. There was a soft knock at the door.

"Come in!"

The door opened, and Donald Clark stood there, looking gray. "Come in, Don, and close the door behind you." She showed him to a sofa and took the one opposite. "First of all, Don, I want to tell you again how sorry we all were to hear of Pat's untimely death."

"Thank you, Madam President," Clark said, lowering his eyes.

"And I want to thank you again for continuing with

your inaugural party after getting the news about Pat. It was a brave thing to do."

"I felt the flow of events shouldn't be disturbed because of a personal tragedy."

"How are you, Don? It's understandable that you don't feel entirely yourself these days."

"I'm muddling through, I guess."

"Well, I don't think you should do that anymore. I think you need some time off and a real rest, and outside of Washington. The press here has been just awful."

"Yes, it has, but I don't think I can take time off at this juncture."

"It's the perfect time, Don, and I don't have to tell you that our prospects for an early confirmation have been dimmed by the press reports. It's all trash, of course, but it has an effect on the Senate."

"I don't understand."

"I'm afraid we can't go forward with your confirmation, given the circumstances. We can't afford to lose a vote so early in the administration."

"You mean . . ."

"Yes, Don, you're going to have to leave, I'm afraid. Now, you go back to New York or to your home in . . . Westport, is it?"

"Greenwich."

"Ah, yes, Greenwich." She stood, forcing him to stand with her. The distant beat of a helicopter's rotors could be heard, growing louder. She took his arm and propelled him toward the outside door, opened it, then into the Rose Garden. An Air Force helicopter set down gently on the White House helipad. Its door opened and an Army sergeant emerged and braced at the door.

Holly kept Clark moving. "There'll be a car waiting at the East Side heliport, to take you wherever you need to go. Keep in touch, and after this issue has been resolved, perhaps we can find another slot for you. In the meantime, please send along your resignation for our files."

He tried to respond, but the rotors drowned him out. Holly handed him off to the sergeant, who ushered him aboard, then entered and closed the door. The machine lifted off and made a climbing turn to the north.

Holly made her way back into the Oval Office and picked up a phone. "Is Kirby Reese here, yet?"

"Yes, Madam President."

"Please send him in."

The door opened, and a short, dapper man in his sixties came in.

"Good morning, Kirby, I hope you're well," Holly said, showing him to the sofa and taking her seat.

"Thank you, yes, Madam President."

"This is the perfect moment to have you here," Holly said. "Perhaps you've heard, we're short a cabinet member."

"No, I hadn't heard."

"Don Clark is, of course, broken up about the death of his wife and feels that he can't accept commerce at this point."

"I'm sorry to hear that," Reese said.

"And so I want to offer you the post of secretary of commerce, and I hope you will accept."

"Thank you, Madam President, I'd be honored to join your cabinet."

"Oh, good." She rose, bringing him to his feet. "Our first cabinet meeting is at three o'clock this afternoon. I'll look forward to seeing you then. My secretary will give you some briefing papers as you leave."

They shook hands, and Reese left.

Holly went back to her study and to work. Once again, all was right with the world. For the moment. She knew that couldn't last. Then she had a thought and buzzed her secretary.

"Yes, Madam President?"

"Will you send in my briefing book for this afternoon's cabinet meeting?"

"Yes, ma'am."

"And is that young lady from Ralph Lauren's office still in town?"

"I believe she leaves for New York this afternoon."

"Could you get her on the phone for me?"

"Of course, Madam President."

A moment later, her phone rang. "Ms. Roth," her secretary said.

Holly picked up the phone. "Shelley?"

"Yes, Madam President."

"I wonder if you could do something for me. I need a dress made for a friend of mine. Her birthday is this weekend. Could your people run something up for me?"

"Of course. What did you have in mind?"

"A burka."

"Did you say a *burka*?"

"I did. She's Muslim. Nothing too colorful, but not black, either. Something that doesn't attract too much attention."

"Shall I send you some swatches?"

"No, I'll trust your judgment."

"What dress size is she?"

"Fortunately, exactly the same as mine; you can use the dummy you made up for me."

"And when do you need it?"

"If you could deliver it to the attention of Claire Dunne—she's the head of my Secret Service detail—at the Carlyle Hotel by noon on Friday."

"Of course."

"And send the bill to my friend Stone Barrington. You have his address. It's a gift from both of us."

"Consider it done, Madam President."

"Goodbye, Shelley." Holly hung up. It would amuse Stone to get the bill, she thought . . .

8

On Friday morning, Joan entered Stone's office and handed him a thick, creamy envelope with the words *Ralph Lauren* printed on the back-flap. "This came for you," she said. "I suppose it's a tailoring bill, but somehow, it doesn't sound like you."

Stone removed the contents of the envelope and scanned it, then burst out laughing. "I didn't think she'd do it," he said.

"Who'd do it?"

"Holly. We can expect her sometime this afternoon. She'll drive straight into the garage."

"I'm confused," Joan said. "In a *burka?*"

"Exactly. It's the only way she can travel around the city without being recognized."

Joan laughed, too. "God, I hope the tabloids don't get wind of this."

"They won't, because you and a Secret Service agent are the only people who know. If the press finds out, we'll know who to shoot."

"Oh, I almost forgot. A Mr. Donald Clark phoned, and he insisted on coming over here immediately. He says you know him."

"We've met," Stone said. "I've met his wife, too. Send him in when he arrives. And send Ralph Lauren a check."

"Will do."

Five minutes later, Joan ushered in Donald Clark.

Stone shook his hand. "Hello, Don. Once again, my condolences."

"Thank you, Stone."

"And thank you for your hospitality on Inauguration Day."

"You're very welcome."

"What brings you to see me, Don?"

"I have a problem, and I hope you can help me with it."

"That depends on the problem."

"You may not have heard, yet, but the president has withdrawn my name for consideration by the Senate for the cabinet office of secretary of commerce."

"I heard," Stone said, not mentioning that he had heard before Clark.

"Her reasons were, first, that I looked tired and should have a rest, far from Washington. And, second, that I was unlikely to have enough support in the Senate for confirmation to a cabinet position."

"Well, for the first, I can confirm that you do look tired, Don, as I would think any normal human being would after being subjected to the treatment that you have received from the media. As for the second reason, I am not a politician, but the president certainly is, and she is advised by political experts. If they see your confirmation by the Senate as a problem, then it is, ipso facto, a problem."

Clark's face reddened. "That is the conventional wisdom, of course," he said.

"Sometimes the conventional wisdom is the best wisdom available," Stone replied. He shrugged. "I'm afraid I can't see how I could be of help to you."

"Here's how: I want to launch a private investigation into my wife's murder. I know that you have a police background, and I'd like you to head the investigation."

"To what effect?"

"To the effect of clearing my name and making me suitable for a cabinet post."

"So you want me to conduct an investigation that clears you of your wife's murder?"

"That is correct."

"Don, an investigation that ends in a preconceived verdict would not be an investigation. It would be a sham, and no honorable attorney or firm would be a part of that. I think what you need is a publicist, what those in Washington like to call a spin doctor. The problem is that preconceived verdict I mentioned. What a publicist can do is to hear your story, read all the news reports, and write a statement for you to deliver to the media— preferably in person—that asserts your claim of innocence. That might dispel some doubts, but not all doubts. Some people are just doubters."

"Then what am I to do?"

"I'm afraid that you will have to wait for the police to

announce the results of their investigation into your wife's murder. It would be very helpful to your cause if they also announced the arrest and charging of a perpetrator—one who is not you."

"So you think that I killed or hired someone to kill my wife?"

"I have not formed an opinion on that subject, not having heard the results of the police investigation," Stone said. "I can tell you, though, that if you, before the police investigation is concluded, make a public declaration of your innocence, then the results of the investigation could turn public opinion against you. My advice is to wait for that announcement, then make a public statement either accepting or denying the results of the investigation. It is likely, though, that a police announcement establishing your guilt will have been preceded by your arrest, so you will have to wait for your arraignment to declare your innocence to the public.

"In the meantime, I advise you to retain a criminal attorney from a distinguished Washington law firm to declare your innocence and to respond to any hint of your guilt. And I'm afraid that is all I can do for you."

They rose simultaneously, and Clark extended his hand. "Thank you for your advice. Please send me your bill."

"Don, you are welcome to my advice, and there is no bill."

Clark turned and walked out of Stone's office.

Joan buzzed Stone. "Dino on line one."

Stone picked up his phone. "You won't believe who just left my office," he said.

"My best guess would be Donald Clark," Dino said.

"How the hell did you know that?"

"Because you are the third attorney in New York that he has spoken to today."

"Are you having him followed?"

"Maybe just the tiniest bit."

"Who . . ." Stone began, then stopped himself. "Never mind, I don't want to know who the other attorneys were."

"I'll give you a hint," Dino said, "they are all sleazier than you."

"Thank you, I think."

"Dinner tonight?" Dino asked.

"I'm afraid I am otherwise occupied."

"Anybody I know?"

"I'll give you a hint," Stone said. "She wears a burka." He hung up, laughing.

9

Late in the afternoon, while Stone was still in his office, the president of the United States, swathed from the tips of her toes to the top of her hair in silk, entered the room and slunk a hip on his desk.

"So? How do I look?"

"I can't tell, because I can't see you."

"Would you like me to take it off?"

"Are you wearing anything under it?"

"Why bother?"

"Then I think you should wait until we're upstairs, because Joan might still be in her office, or there might be a Secret Service agent wandering about."

"No problem with them. I've banished them from the interior of the house. Joan, on the other hand . . ."

Stone took her hand, which was clad in a white silk glove, and walked her to the elevator. He gazed into the one open space on her body. "I think I had forgotten how lovely your eyes are," he said. She unfastened something at her throat, revealing her face, and they kissed until the elevator door opened and he led her to the master bedroom.

"Is there a rip cord, or something?" he asked.

Apparently there was, because she did something, and the garment fell into a puddle at her feet.

Stone was able to undress quickly, because she was helping, and they fell into bed together.

"At last, a woman again," she said, "and not a president."

A muffled ringing noise came from somewhere in the room. "I told them not to call me, unless there was a dire emergency," she said.

"Then you'd better answer," Stone replied.

She got out of bed, found her handbag, got back into bed with her phone, then answered it. "This better be very, very bad or very, very good," she said, then listened, her face a blank.

"Shoot him," she said, then listened again for a moment. "Oblige him. Or her. Anything else? Good. Issue a statement from me and keep it cool." She hung up.

"What?" Stone asked.

"Somehow, a man with an assault rifle got onto the White House grounds and fired several rounds at the building. No one hurt, no windows broken."

"And you had to tell them to shoot him?"

"They think his intention may be suicide by Secret Service agent."

"And that was what 'oblige him' was about?"

"Yes," she said. "Where were we?"

Stone rapidly found his place again, and they continued.

Sometime later, they dozed off for a few minutes, then Holly said, "Were you planning dinner in your study?"

"Either there or here," Stone replied. "What is your preference?"

"Here, please. It's so much closer to you."

Stone rang downstairs for dinner, and in due course, food was sent up on the dumbwaiter. He tasted the wine, then looked at the label. "Ah," he said, "this is one of those beautiful reds Marcel DuBois gave me: a Château Palmer, '61. Fit for a president."

"Absolutely marvelous," Holly said, sipping some. "All we have in the White House cellars are American wines, and I love them, especially the cabernets, but I miss French wines."

They were quiet for a while, then Stone said, "Donald Clark came to see me today."

"Whatever for?" Holly asked.

"He wanted me to conduct an investigation into his wife's murder and proclaim him innocent of all charges."

"What did you tell him?"

"To get stuffed. In the nicest possible way, of course."

"How did he take that?"

"He took it somewhere else. Dino told me I was the third lawyer he'd talked to today. Apparently, the NYPD is keeping an eye on him."

"After what you told me about his threesomes with Little Debby Myers and a girlfriend, I think it's a good thing that I got him out the door immediately."

"The man is a ticking time bomb," Stone said.

"Then why won't he just go away quietly and write his memoirs? Or hire someone to do so?"

"Maybe he thinks his life isn't interesting enough for an autobiography."

"*Everybody* thinks his—or her—life is interesting enough for an autobiography," Holly said, "if they just had the time to write it."

"Well, I guess Don has nothing but time, now, but all he wants is to clear his name."

"I think he had Pat killed," Holly said.

"Really?"

"He had motive: a bad and very expensive divorce. Means: enough money to hire an assassin. And opportunity: an alibi."

"I missed the alibi."

"His mother; you met her at the inaugural party, remember?"

"Now I remember," Stone said. "I don't think the word of one's mother is sufficient for a credible alibi—especially one as old as the elder Mrs. Clark. She's got to be in her nineties."

"Ninety-seven," she said. "At that age, there's always dementia, or just plain forgetfulness, to consider."

"Both my parents lived into their mid-nineties," Stone said, "and they were as sharp as tacks, until the day they died."

"I didn't speak with her long enough to get an impression," Holly said. "Still, Little Debby's homicide people bought the alibi."

"You think Debby may have put her thumb on the scale?" Stone asked.

"Given her position, it's a pretty big thumb," Holly pointed out. "There's a tiny part of my brain that is still a cop," she said, "so I'm always a skeptic about alibis."

"I guess I'm a softer touch than you," Stone said. "I tend to believe them, until I have a reason not to."

"Little Debby certainly got Art out of town in a hurry, didn't she?"

"Yes, and he seemed baffled about New York, said this was the first time he'd been here."

"Well," Holly said, "I guess not every American has visited the Big Apple."

Stone put their dishes back on the cart and into the dumbwaiter. "Would you like some dessert?" he asked.

"Yes, I would."

"We've got some ice cream downstairs."

"I didn't mean that kind of dessert," she said, fondling him.

10

Stone awoke at seven, and Holly and her burka were gone. He had just sat up in bed and rung for breakfast when his cell phone rang. Blocked call. "Yes?"

"It is I. I'm sorry to dematerialize so soon, but I have a nine o'clock, and I can't do that in a burka."

"Understood. Tonight?"

"Let me see what I can do." She hung up. Stone sighed.

She rang back after ten minutes. "I've just been told that I have an afternoon of appointments," she said, "and a dinner."

"Oh, well."

"I think what I'll have to do is plan further ahead and blank out a couple of days as vacation time."

"Then the press will want to know where you're going."

"I'll take a firm line on that. They'll get used to it."

"What happened to the man with the rifle?"

"They shot him, but not dead. Sounds like he'll end up in a mental ward for a long rest."

"You were safer in my arms," he said.

"Don't I know it! Gotta run." She hung up.

Stone had just sat down at his desk when Joan buzzed him. "Dino on one."

Stone pushed the button. "Good morning."

"You obviously haven't seen the early edition of the *New York Post*."

"I try to spare myself that."

"There's what you might call a speculative, not to say a made-up, story that a woman in a burka was spotted leaving the Carlyle with a known Secret Service agent."

"Oh, shit."

"It's okay, they think she had a Muslim visitor. They're working that up into a brink-of-war-in-the-Middle-East story."

"Whew!"

"Nice idea, though. Whose was it?"

"Hers, I think. I can't remember."

"I think you're going to have to think up a better story, one that takes place in a less convenient place. How about Camp David?"

"Lots of staff around there."

"Some other place where you have a house?"

"Too cold in Maine, too far to L.A., England, or France, unless there's legit government business in one of those."

"Problem is, after all that waltzing on inaugural

night, you're now officially on the radar, not to mention fair game."

"Tell me about it."

"Maybe what Holly needs is a beard."

"That would be unattractive."

"You know what I mean: a harmless male escort, preferably gay and out of the closet."

"I don't know how that would work. The problem is, eventually, we're going to get busted. And it will be worse than if we had just made an announcement after the inauguration."

"How about an engagement announcement in the Sunday *Times*?"

"Engaged for eight years?"

"Well, there is that. Plus, you'll never get laid again, if people believe you are engaged to the president. Of course, there's a certain kind of woman who would view that as a challenge."

"Spare me that kind of woman," Stone said.

"If we put our minds together, we could come up with something that would work. Dinner tonight?"

"Patroon, at seven," Stone said, then hung up. He asked Joan to book the table.

He was halfway through a bourbon before Dino showed. Half a dozen people had complimented him on his waltzing.

Dino slid into the booth, just ahead of a Johnnie

Walker Black on the rocks. "Did you come up with anything yet?" Stone asked.

"I haven't given it a thought."

"Me, either."

"How about moving to another city?"

"It would have to be London or Paris. I can't buy any more houses. And I'd never see Holly again."

"Presidents visit London and Paris."

"I don't think I can conduct a sexual relationship while accompanied by a motorcycle escort," Stone said.

"Yeah, I guess that kind of travel would entail an entourage."

"Look who's here," Stone said, nodding toward the entrance.

Dino looked. "Well, as I live and breathe. Our Lieutenant Jacoby has found a restaurant table in New York."

Jacoby was with an attractive brunette, Stone noted. "A table isn't all he's found."

Jacoby saw them across the room and nodded. He ordered a drink, then excused himself from the brunette and crossed to their booth. Hands were shaken.

"I want to ask your advice," he said.

"Which one of us?" Dino asked.

"Both of you. I had a visit this afternoon from Donald Clark."

Stone threw up a hand. "Wait, wait, don't tell me. He wants you to conduct an investigation of his wife's murder and find him innocent."

"You, too?"

"Everybody in town," Stone said.

"Did you give him any advice?"

"Yes, I told him to go back to D.C., hire a top criminal lawyer from a top firm, and have him issue a statement that he's innocent."

"I guess that's cheaper than an investigation," Jacoby said.

"I guess so. What advice did you give him?"

"I told him it was ethically inappropriate for him to seek my advice, since I'm still listed as an investigating officer on the case."

"I like it," Stone said.

"Enjoy your dinner," Jacoby said. "Any recommendations?"

"The chateaubriand or the Dover sole," Stone said. "Or anything else. It's all good."

Jacoby gave him a little salute and returned to his brunette. "I wonder who else is on the list," Stone said.

"Sherlock Holmes," Dino replied.

11

Stone's phone was ringing as he walked into his bedroom. "Hello?"

"It's Eggers." Bill Eggers had been a law school classmate of Stone's and was managing partner of Woodman & Weld, the prestigious law firm in which Stone was a senior partner.

"Hello, Bill. It's a little late. Do you need bail money?"

"Har de har," Eggers said. "I need a traveling companion who owns a Gulfstream 500."

"Have you been reduced to hitchhiking?" Stone asked.

"No, but I need to fly to L.A. tomorrow morning for a couple of days. The firm's airplane is in the shop, undergoing an inspection of some sort, and I need one of the firm's attorneys to accompany me, so naturally I chose the one who has a Gulfstream."

"Naturally. What time do you want wheels up?"

"Ten AM. I'm not an early riser. The firm will pay for the use of the aircraft and all expenses, of course."

"You mean, one or more of the firm's clients is paying?"

"Same thing. You in?"

"Why not. There's room in my house for you."

"Thanks, but I've taken a large suite. There'll be meetings all day the day after tomorrow."

"For which my attendance will be required?"

"Only one meeting for that. I'll explain on the way."

"Be aboard by nine-forty-five," Stone said, then hung up. He called his pilot, Faith Barnacle. "You'll need a copilot and a stewardess," he explained, "and catering for two of us and the crew—lunch and an afternoon snack. Wheels up at ten AM. I'll do the takeoff and landing."

"Do I get to know where we're going?" Faith asked.

"Sorry, L.A. You can call the Arrington and arrange your usual rooms. Also, request transportation for two. There'll be a guest aboard. Get yourself a rental car for the crew."

"How many days away?"

"At least a couple."

"See you tomorrow."

The following morning, Stone was driven by his factotum, Fred Flicker, to Teterboro Airport, across the river in New Jersey. He needed only a briefcase, since he had a wardrobe at the L.A. house, which was situated on the grounds of the Arrington, a hotel named for his late wife. When he boarded the Gulfstream, Bill Eggers was already there, sipping something that looked suspiciously like a gin and tonic.

"It's club soda," Eggers said, suspecting Stone's suspicions and waving him to a seat. The stewardess closed and locked the main cabin door and greeted them. "Coffee, tea, or anything else?" she asked. The sound of engines starting followed her.

"Tea," Stone replied, and she brought a little pot and a cup.

"Tea?" Eggers said. "Really?"

"I've already had a strong cup of coffee this morning, and I don't require further caffeination," Stone explained. He sweetened the tea and squeezed lemon into it. "Also, I'm doing the takeoff and landing, and the FAA frowns on, ah, club soda, before flying." He drank his tea as they taxied, then went forward and took the left seat from Faith, while she displaced her copilot from the right seat.

She read out the checklist to him, and he followed it meticulously. "The clearance is already loaded into the FMS," Faith said, referring to the computer called the flight management system. Stone was given a takeoff clearance by the tower as he approached the runway; he didn't even have to slow down to make the turn. He moved the throttles forward to the takeoff position and used the tiller to get the aircraft on the center line, then switched to the rudder pedals, when they had enough ground speed for the rudder to be effective. He rotated, and the airplane climbed. Stone performed the departure procedures, then turned over the controls to Faith and her copilot and resumed his seat in the cabin.

"Okay," he said to Eggers. "We're flying. What's up?"

"Do you remember a man named Edgar Wheelis?" Bill asked.

"Vaguely," Stone said.

"I'm going to wrap up negotiations with him for a piece of property in L.A., and I want you at the meeting."

"Why?" Stone asked.

"Because Edgar is afraid of you."

"Of me? Why?"

"I don't know, and I don't care to know," Eggers said. "All I know is that, if you're at the meeting, I'll get everything I want from Edgar."

"I don't recall ever having been used as a threat," Stone said. "I'm just a mild-mannered attorney-at-law, with a winning way about him."

"Especially *winning*, where Edgar is concerned," Bill replied. Then he opened his *Wall Street Journal* and began to read, ignoring Stone.

Stone took a novel from his briefcase and read until lunch was served. Later, as they neared the landing at Burbank, Stone went forward and took the controls, hand-flying the arrival procedures and the ILS, the instrument landing system. He needed to keep his hand in and his logbook up to date.

A Bentley, one of the fleet from the Arrington, met them at Burbank and drove them to the hotel. Eggers was dropped at the main entrance, then Stone was driven to his house, at the rear of the hotel property. He had negotiated the land sale for his late wife, who had inherited it from her first husband, the film star Vance Calder, who had included the building of the house for her in the contract. When she was murdered by a former lover, Stone had inherited it, along with a chunk of her estate. The bulk of the estate went to a trust for their son, Peter.

Stone left his suit to be pressed by the butler, stripped, got into a terry-cloth robe, and walked down to the house's pool, which was surrounded by a high hedge. He could hear splashing from the pool, which was odd, because it was private. Probably somebody's dog having a swim, he thought.

He entered through the gate and immediately saw a two-piece swimsuit lying on a chaise.

"Excuse me," a woman's voice said from the other end. "This is a private pool."

"I'm aware of that," Stone said pleasantly, "since it belongs to me."

"Oh. Does that mean I'm the interloper here?"

"That's too strong a term. Let's just call you an unexpected guest. Do you mind if I join you?"

"All right, but I warn you, I'm naked."

"That's all right," Stone said, "so am I." He shucked off the robe and dived into the water.

12

Stone got a glimpse of a very nice body before he surfaced, a polite distance from her.

"I'm Lara Parks," she said.

"And I'm Stone Barrington."

"Are you in the film business?"

"On the edges of it, you might say. I'm an attorney. Are you in the film business?"

"I suppose you could say I'm on the edges, too. Heretofore, I've done only television."

"But you have designs on feature films?"

She laughed. "Yes, I have designs."

"Then I wish you luck."

"One always needs a little luck. I have an appointment tomorrow with a director named Peter Barrington . . . Any relation?"

"Yes, he's my son. And this hotel is named for his mother."

"May I tell him I know you?"

"If you do, he will take that as knowledge of a wild

affair between us. Anyway, you already have an appointment with him; that's the hard part. All you have to do now is to show him you can act."

"And how would I do that?"

"It's called an audition, I believe."

"He called it a reading. I think there will be other actors there, too."

"Good, you won't be all alone."

"Any advice?"

"I'm in no position to advise you, but I'll tell you a story that an old friend of mine, who was a producer and director, told me. He and the head of the studio had a meeting with a young actor who was very assertive, unlike most actors, who are nervous on such occasions. The studio head grilled him about the part and his interpretation, and he gave smart-ass answers. My friend suddenly realized that the actor wasn't just chatting; he was acting the character he had been called in to audition for. He got the part."

"That was very clever," she said. "Risky, too. I wonder if I could pull that off?"

"I wonder, too, but I don't know. It's just something to consider, especially if the studio head is at the meeting. Directors are smarter about such things."

"Now I don't know what to do."

"Study your lines and give them your best reading," Stone said.

"Now *that* is good advice. You don't look old enough to be Peter Barrington's father."

"That means either that Peter is younger than you

think, or I'm older than I look. Either way, it was the right thing to say."

They were quiet for a moment.

"Is Lara Parks your real name, or did someone suggest it to you?"

"My parents are Swiss, and the name they gave me was Helga Glick. *Everyone* suggested I change it, so I made up Lara Parks."

"Has anyone ever asked you if you're related to Larry Parks?"

"No. I've never heard of him."

"He was a talented actor in the forties and fifties, but he ran afoul of a congressional committee investigation into communism in the movie business . . . He was blacklisted, as a result, and didn't work in films for several years, so the correct answer to that question, as well as the truthful one, is no."

"I'll google him, so I'll know what I'm talking about."

Stone looked at his Rolex. "I believe the sun is over the yardarm, as they say. Would you like a drink?"

"Yes, I would. May I have a vodka and tonic, please?"

"Of course." Stone swam to the other end of the pool, climbed out, put on his robe, picked up a phone, and ordered. Then he picked up Lara's robe, took it to a ladder, and held it open for her, screening his view.

She climbed out and slipped into it. "Thank you for being so nice, but I'm not shy."

"I'll keep that in mind," Stone replied, offering her a seat. The butler appeared with their drinks and left them to it.

"Have you ever been asked not to be shy when auditioning?"

"Yes. When that happens, I become shy. Have you ever noticed that the biggest female stars seem never to show so much as a nipple?"

"I have noticed that. There must be a reason."

"I think the reasoning is: leave them wanting more."

Stone laughed. "I expect that's good advice."

"I'm surprised that you haven't made a pass at me."

"Are you free for dinner this evening?"

"Yes."

"Then come to my house at seven, and the cook will cook for us. I promise to be on my worst behavior."

She laughed. "I'll hold you to that. Now, I have to go. They're sending a hairdresser over to do me up for to-morrow."

"The studio?"

"Yes."

"And they put you up in this hotel?"

"Apparently, they keep a cottage for out-of-town guests."

"I'd say you're getting star treatment."

"I could get used to that," she said. She kissed him on the forehead and walked away.

He was napping on his bed when the phone rang. "Yes?"

"Dad? It's Peter."

"How are you?" Stone asked.

"Just fine. Will you dine with us tonight?"

"I'm afraid I already have plans. I'm sorry."

"Can't you bring her with you?"

"I'm afraid not. I'll explain it all later. I'll be here for a few days, so we'll find time."

"As you wish." They caught up a bit, then hung up. Stone had a shower and a shave and got dressed, in preparation of being on his worst behavior. His phone rang. "Hello?"

"Hi, it's Lara Parks."

"Good evening."

"Tell me, did you mean what you said?"

"My recollection is that I didn't say much, but I meant all of it."

"I'd prefer it if you were on your best behavior, rather than your worst."

"Granted. Would you like to put another quarter in the machine?"

"See you at seven," she said, then hung up.

13

Promptly at seven, the doorbell rang, and the butler answered it.

Stone arrived downstairs a moment later and found Lara Parks seated in a chair before the fireplace with a drink in her hand and a magazine in her lap.

"Good evening," he said, shaking her hand. His bourbon was already resting on the chairside table, and he sat down.

"You didn't tell me about this," she said accusingly, holding up the magazine.

Stone peered at the publication. "I believe it's a copy of *People* magazine. I believe this, because it says *People* at the top."

"Please tell me how this came to be."

Stone took a swig of his drink and drew a breath. "Well, many years ago—I forget exactly how many—*Time* magazine had a weekly column called *People* that offered tidbits of gossip about movie stars and such. It proved so popular among readers that they inflated it into an actual weekly magazine, and it became very popular."

"You know that's not what I mean."

"Did I misidentify the magazine? I admit I haven't read it for years, but it did have that name on the cover."

"Yes, but it's not what I *mean*."

"I'm sorry, I'm baffled," Stone said. "What *did* you mean?"

"You know."

"Am I meant to divine your thoughts? If so, I'm not doing very well."

"I mean *this*," she said, opening the magazine and holding it up with both hands, displaying a double-page color photograph of Stone waltzing with Holly Barker.

"I hadn't seen that," Stone said.

She remained silent, glaring at him.

"Really," he said, "I hadn't seen it until this moment."

"How did you miss it?" she demanded.

"By the simple device of not reading the magazine, which you have thoughtfully done for me. I also didn't read the newspapers the following morning, and I instructed my secretary to keep all knowledge of such from me."

"Why?"

"Because I didn't want to have conversations like this one. You seem to have taken it as a personal affront that I have not raised the subject of the inaugural night. Why is that?"

"Because it makes me feel like a fool."

"I'm sorry, that just doesn't make any sense," Stone said.

"You should have told me who you were, instead of leaving me to find out for myself."

"I beg your pardon, I believe I answered each of your questions fully and honestly. If more than that is required of me, please ask me more questions."

"All right. How did you come to be waltzing with the president on inaugural night?"

"We are old friends, and she invited me to escort her."

"And you are 'just good friends'? I believe the saying is?"

"No, we are *very* good friends," he replied. "She chose the waltz."

"Are you sleeping with her?"

"I think the most acceptable answer to that question is 'None of your business,' which would also be the answer if someone asked it about you."

Lara made an odd, strangling noise, then threw the magazine into the fireplace.

"If that magazine belonged to the Arrington, then I will have to report you to the management for destroying hotel property," Stone said.

Finally, she laughed. "You would be within your rights to do so," she said.

"And you are within your rights to ask for another drink," Stone replied.

"Same again," she said.

He spoke those words into the phone and another round arrived.

She sipped hers. "Would it be an intrusion if I ask how you know Holly Barker?"

"No, but it's a complicated story, probably requiring another drink."

"Go ahead," she said. "I can take it."

"Some years ago I was in Vero Beach, Florida, to accept delivery of a new airplane from the manufacturer Piper Aircraft, whose factory is there. I had transferred the funds to a bank, in a neighboring town called Orchid Beach, and I went there to obtain a cashier's check for the amount owed on delivery. While I was waiting in line, some people wearing masks and bearing shotguns entered the bank and shouted at everybody—the sorts of things you've seen on television: 'Shut up, give us the money,' et cetera.

"In their haste to be done with their work, they roughed up a woman who had had the temerity to ask them what they thought they were doing. They knocked her down with a shotgun butt. The man standing behind me in line made to ward them off and help her, and received a shotgun blast to his chest for his trouble. I did my best to help him, but he died before the ambulance arrived, about three minutes later, as did the police.

"They asked the customers not to leave until they were questioned, so I was present for some time, during which the chief of police arrived and identified the body as that of her fiancé, to whom, I later learned, she was to be married the following day. She stayed on to help question the people in the bank, among them, me. Her name was Holly Barker. She gave me her card and asked me to call her if I thought of anything else, and I gave her mine. About three months later I went back to the Piper factory on airplane business, and I invited her to lunch. We've been friends ever since."

"What about the robbers? Were they caught?"

"That's a much longer story, with more details than I can remember, but someone wrote a book about it called *Orchid Beach*, and I'm sure the concierge can get a copy for you."

The butler entered the room and announced dinner, so they moved to a table that had been set for them.

They dined slowly, getting along well. As the dishes were taken away after dessert, Lara said, "I apologize for shouting at you. I had begun to think that I was the victim of a practical joke, what with my meeting tomorrow with your son."

"Peter is not in on the joke, so I wouldn't mention it to him."

"All right, don't rub it in."

"If you'll pardon me for reverting to my original intentions, that sounds like a very good idea," Stone said.

"Yes, it does," she replied.

14

Stone woke early, to the sound of the shower running. Lara appeared shortly with one towel wrapped around her and another around her head. "Do you have a hair dryer?" she asked.

"Cupboard under the sink," he replied, and she vanished. While she dried her hair, he got shaved and showered.

"Breakfast?" he asked her.

"What time is it?"

"Seven-thirty."

"Two eggs over easy, bacon, English muffin, OJ, coffee," she replied.

Stone called it in on the bathroom phone, then dried his own hair.

She reached over and undid the towel around his waist. "You look good naked," she said.

He did the same for her. "You, too."

"Quickie?"

"I don't think we'll be quick enough, with breakfast on the way. Rain check?"

"Sure, even if it's not raining."

They were propped up in bed in time for the arrival of breakfast. While they were eating, Stone's phone rang. "Hello?"

"Dad, it's Peter. Lunch at the studio today?"

"You buying?"

Peter laughed. "You betcha."

"Then we're on."

"Noon, at my bungalow," he said.

"See you then."

Stone turned to Lara. "What time is your appointment at Centurion?"

"Ten-thirty."

"I'll give you a lift, then. I'm having lunch with Peter after you're done."

"Thanks, but they're sending a car for me at ten."

They finished breakfast, and the butler took away the debris. "Where were we?" he asked.

"What time is it?"

"Eight-ten."

She climbed on top of him. "I like being on top," she said.

"I like you being on top," he replied, rising to the occasion.

She did the rest.

Stone arrived at Peter's bungalow at Centurion Studios at noon.

"Good morning, Mr. Barrington," the receptionist

said. "He's in a meeting, be done shortly. Why don't you have a seat in the garden?"

Stone strolled out back and took a chaise longue next to a fountain. The garden was soft and lovely, something new at the bungalow. He was about to doze off when voices woke him. He looked up to see Peter and his production partner, Ben Bacchetti, Dino's son, walking into the garden with a young man and a young woman.

Stone and Peter hugged, then Stone and Ben.

"Dad," Peter said, "this is Jeff Tatum and Lara Parks, the stars of our new film."

Stone shook Jeff's hand, then Lara's. "Congratulations to both of you," he said.

"Your father and I have met," Lara said to Peter. "We're neighbors at the Arrington."

"Good. Dad, we've just invited these folks to dinner at our house," Peter said. "Why don't you join us?"

"What a good idea," Stone said.

"Unfortunately, they both have plans for lunch, so say goodbye."

"Goodbye," Stone said, winking at Lara.

She winked back, and they left.

"Don't tell me," Peter said.

"Tell you what?"

"Never mind."

"Bad news," Peter said. "Leo Goldman is on his deathbed." Goldman was the chairman and CEO of Centurion.

"I'm sorry to hear it. Leo's a good man."

"Yes," Peter said, "he is. We're planning to visit him

in the hospice after lunch. Would you like to come with us?"

"Yes, I've always liked Leo, and I liked his father before him."

"I, as well. But Ben is going to make a better CEO. Can we get him elected?"

"Well, if we put together my shares, your trust's shares, Ben's shares, and Strategic Service's shares, we'll have a narrow majority, I think. Congratulations, Ben."

Ben threw up his hands. "Let's not get ahead of ourselves," he said. "Bad luck."

"You make your own luck," Stone said. "Both of you always have."

Stone's phone went off and he looked at it for the caller: Dino. "It's your old man," he said to Ben. "Excuse me for a moment. Hello, Dino."

"Yeah. You, too."

"I'm with your son and mine."

"Great, do you . . ."

"Did you hear that Leo Goldman is in the twilight of his life?"

"Yeah? Does that mean . . ."

"It does. You won't have to support Ben anymore."

That got a big laugh from Ben, whose income was a dozen times that of his father's.

"Shut up and listen," Dino said.

"I'm listening."

"Art Jacoby, the detective from D.C. . . ."

"I remember."

"I told you to shut up and listen."

Stone said nothing.

"Hello? Are you there?"

"I'm following instructions," Stone said.

"Okay, anyway, some guys from DCPD showed up here ten minutes ago with a warrant for his arrest."

"On what charge?"

"I told you to shut up."

Stone shut up.

"Are you there?"

Stone said nothing.

"He's charged, along with his girlfriend, with the murder of Patricia Clark."

"May I speak now?"

"Yeah, go ahead."

"Wow."

"That's all you've got to say?"

"Is this the girlfriend who was part of the three-some?"

"Yeah."

"I have nothing else to say." Dino hung up.

15

They finished a good lunch, then Peter's secretary came outside. "Leo Goldman's assistant called. Leo died a few minutes ago."

There was an audible groan from everybody.

"Send some nice flowers to his house," Peter said. "I don't suppose we know anything about the funeral arrangements yet."

"We know that Leo planned every detail of the funeral. The memorial service will be held in the executive auditorium, at three PM tomorrow, burial afterward at the little graveyard on the back lot, where studio VIPs rest, next to his father."

"Fine," Peter said.

Ben spoke up. "Make a note that when I kick off, I'm not to be buried there. I spent enough time in the boardroom with those guys."

"Me, too," Peter said. "Dad, where do you want to be buried?"

"I really haven't given it any thought, but I'd like to

be scattered, not buried, from the afterdeck of *Breeze*, within sight of my house in Dark Harbor, and anybody who won't make the trip to Maine is no friend of mine. You can have a memorial service in New York, to give them an excuse for not coming."

"You haven't given it any thought at all, then?" Peter said.

"Not much."

On the way home, Stone's phone rang. "Yes?"

"It's Lara. Now that I've got the job they're kicking me out of the Arrington first thing tomorrow morning. I'm not looking forward to going back to my little apartment in Santa Monica."

"So, why don't you move in with me?" Stone suggested. "I'll be here a little longer."

"I was hoping you'd say that. Yes, please."

"Don't wait for tomorrow. Pack, and I'll send the butler over there for your luggage as soon as I get home."

"I'll need all of fifteen minutes," she replied. "Bye."

As she hung up, Stone's phone rang again. "Yes?"

"It's Dino. Shut up and listen."

Stone sighed.

"Okay, Art Jacoby can't get a decent lawyer."

"Indigent?"

"No, shunned. Word has apparently gotten out through Little Debby. Any ideas?"

"Yeah. Where are they holding Art?"

"DCPD detention."

"I'll see what I can do." Stone hung up and called Herbie Fisher, a young partner at Woodman & Weld.

"Herb Fisher."

"It's Stone. You had a case that required you to qualify for practicing in D.C., didn't you?"

"Yep," Herbie said. "I'm still good to practice there. What happened, Holly get arrested?"

"No, she's still a free woman, but she might as well be a prisoner, since she's being held in Secret Service detention. There's a guy named Art Jacoby, who . . ."

"I know him. He worked the case I was trying down there."

"He's been arrested for the murder of Patricia Clark."

"Wow."

"Yeah. I've gotten to know him, and I think it's bullshit. You know Little Debby Myers?"

"Who doesn't?"

"She and Donald Clark have been part of a threesome in the past."

"Wow again. So you think he's being framed?"

"Maybe, or maybe they're just rattling his cage, to show him who's in charge. They transferred him to New York, to get him out of the way, but he was still talking—to Dino and me. I'm sure there'll be photographers waiting at the police helipad in D.C."

"Okay, I'll get a guy over there right now to deal with bail, and I'll be in D.C. first thing tomorrow morning. I've got a thing I have to deal with here today."

"Good enough. Let Joan know if Art needs bail money." Stone hung up.

Lara was upstairs unpacking in the women's dressing room in the master suite. She gave him a big kiss. "How was your lunch?"

"Fine. You know who Leo Goldman Jr. is?"

"Head of the studio? He wasn't at our meeting."

"He died while we were having lunch. He had been in a hospice for a couple of days."

"I never met him, but I saw his name in the trades a lot."

"Leo, like his father, liked to get his name in print."

"What does that mean for Peter and Ben? I liked them. I hope Goldman's death is not a problem for them."

"It's more of an opportunity, really. We'll probably get Ben elected CEO at the next board meeting."

"Do you have something to do with that?"

"I'm on the board, and I'm sure we can muster enough shareholders' votes to get the board to appoint Ben. He's pretty much been doing the job while Leo has been sick."

"Good for Ben. What about Peter?"

"What's good for Ben is good for Peter. They've been partners since they were kids. I don't think Peter wants more executive work to do. He just wants to direct, and Ben still produces his pictures."

Lara stripped down to nothing. "What should I wear this evening?"

"I like that outfit," Stone said.

"I'm glad to hear it."

"But for dinner, I guess something casually elegant."

"I'll aim for that."

"There are some good shops in the hotel. Have a look over there, and charge whatever you like to me."

"Wonderful." She took his hand and led him to the bed, then started undressing him. "I need a new agent. You know anybody?"

"Probably. Who's representing you now?"

"A guy named Guy Baxter is telling everybody he is, except he's not."

"Explain."

"Somebody sent me to see him a couple of weeks ago, and he tried to get me to sign a contract, but I wouldn't. I found him creepy. And if I think that, the studios probably do, too." She curled up next to him and put her head on his shoulder.

"Did he arrange the appointment with Peter?"

"No, he didn't even know about it. Jeff Tatum, my new leading man, told Peter about me, and they called. Jeff's represented by a guy at CAA."

"Who sent you to see this Guy Baxter?"

"A bartender at the Beverly Hills Hotel. I was having a drink with a girlfriend, and he waved Guy over and said, 'This girl needs an agent.'"

"That was it?"

"All of it. Guy actually called Peter and asked to introduce me to him, but Peter smelled a rat, I think. I already had the appointment by that time, anyway."

"Well, you want to get that out before your casting hits the trades," Stone said. "When you're done doing what you're doing, write down his name and address, and I'll dictate a letter to him, warning him off."

"I think I'll be finished very, very soon," she said.

"I think you will, too," Stone said.

16

Stone called Joan. "Take a letter, to one Guy Baxter:

Dear Mr. Baxter,

I am the attorney for Lara Parks, who has heard that you've been telling people that you represent her as an agent.

You do not represent her, nor has she authorized you to tell anyone that you do.

I am directed by Ms. Parks to tell you that, unless you cease and desist, forthwith, she will bring a legal action against you and send a copy of the writ to the various trade publications.

"Et cetera, et cetera. Then forge my signature, which you're good at, and fax it to"—he held out his hand, and Lara gave him the agent's card—"Guy Baxter." He gave her the number.

"Got it. Anybody I know?"

"No, but you will. She's the star of Peter's new film."

"I'll have the fax out of here in ten minutes."

"Bye." Stone hung up.

"That sounded good," Lara said.

"He may not give up. If he calls, don't argue with him. Just tell him he does not represent you, then hang up."

"Right." She started dressing. By the time she had finished, her phone was ringing. "Hello? Listen to me very carefully, Mr. Baxter. You do not now nor have you ever represented me in any fashion." She hung up. "You were right," she said to Stone.

Immediately, Stone's phone started to ring. He looked at his phone. "It's Baxter. My secretary must have used a letterhead with this number on it. "Hello."

"Mr. Barrington?"

"Speaking."

"This is Guy Baxter, Lara Parks's agent."

"I said in my letter all that I have to say to you."

"Did she tell you she signed a contract with me?"

"She did not, because she has not done so."

"I'll send you a copy," he said. "You're at the Arrington, right?"

"Goodbye, Mr. Baxter." He hung up and turned to Lara. "Did you sign anything when you were in Baxter's office?"

"Nothing at all."

"Good."

"Oh, he asked me for my autograph; I gave him that."

"What kind of paper?"

"A blank sheet." Her face fell. "Oh, God."

"This complicates things. He's going to send me a contract—a very unfavorable one, I suspect—and it will have your signature on it."

"No, it won't," she said.

"You didn't sign your name?"

"I gave him my autograph," she said. "Not my signature. They're different."

"How so?"

"My autograph is sort of swirling, and carefully written, to be legible. My signature, as on the checks I write, is smaller, faster, and pretty much illegible."

"I'm relieved to hear it," Stone said. They got into an Arrington Bentley and were approaching the gate when a guard flagged them down. He rapped on Stone's window.

"Yes?" Stone asked, rolling it down.

"Delivery for you, Mr. Barrington," he said.

"Thank you." Stone ripped open the envelope and switched on the reading lamp. "It's the contract," he said, leafing through it. "He says he's not only your agent, but your personal manager, and that you're paying him fifteen percent for agenting and twenty-five percent for managing, which includes signing your checks and paying your bills." He showed her the contract. "Is that your signature or your autograph?"

"It's my autograph," Lara replied. "I can show you

other examples of it on my head shots that I send out with replies to fan mail."

"You get fan mail?"

"I'm on TV. I don't get a lot of mail, but enough to have the pictures printed with my autograph on them. The network sends them out; it saves me a lot of time."

"What are you on, on TV?"

"A series called *Trust Me*, which is in the last of its four seasons. We shot the final two episodes last month, and they haven't run yet."

Stone called Joan. "Follow up to the fax," he said.

Dear Mr. Baxter,

Your so-called contract bears Ms. Parks's autograph, which is sent out to thousands of fans of her TV show by the network. This is not her legal signature and, as you know, her autograph is on a blank sheet of paper, which you have used to compose a fraudulent contract. This will be the first exhibit in her lawsuit against you, and I will see that the ethical standards committee of the bar association receives a copy of the contract, along with an autographed photograph.

"Thanks, Joan. Please get it out right away."

"Will do."

Stone hung up. "Lara, do you have an agent presently?"

"I did, but he retired a couple of weeks ago. I haven't had time to look for a new one, and at the end of a series and before you get cast in something else is not the best time to look."

They arrived at Peter's house and were greeted by Peter, his wife, Ben, and Ben's wife.

"Let me show you something," Stone said, after they had sat down with a drink. He handed Baxter's contract to Peter.

Peter scanned it. "This is awful," he said. "I'm surprised any actor would sign such a thing." He handed it to Ben.

"Lara didn't sign it. She gave him her autograph—on a blank sheet of paper—and he hung the contract on it."

"Terrible," Ben agreed.

"I have a question for you both," Stone said. "If you were an actress with an offer in hand for a film, who would you want as an agent?"

They looked at each other and, simultaneously, said, "Arlene Summers."

"She's a partner in a medium-sized agency called the Talent Stable."

"I'd love to be with Arlene Summers," Lara said.

"I'll call her in the morning," Peter said. "I think you two would get along." He handed her the Baxter contract. "Show her this, and tell her how it came to be."

"I'll do that," Lara said, tucking the contract into her handbag.

"I don't see a lot of this sort of thing," Ben said, "but I know it happens. Baxter is going to be looking for a payoff to let her out of this."

"He won't get it," Stone said. "I've already told him we're suing and reporting him to the bar association."

"I'll bet they already have a thick file on him," Ben said. "I'll look into that tomorrow."

They were called to dinner, and the conversation changed.

17

The phone woke Stone at 6:30 AM. "What?"

"Stone, it's Herb, good morning."

"It's three hours earlier out here."

"Oh, dammit, I forgot. Anyway, Art Jacoby is out on bail—five hundred grand's worth, courtesy of Joan."

Stone groaned. "Don't let him flee," he said.

"I've read him the riot act on that possibility. He knows the score. And he knows he won't be convicted, given his alibi, so he has no reason to flee."

"Did they arrest his girlfriend?"

"No."

"Then you might move her somewhere, in case they get ideas. I don't want to have to shell out any more bail money. Are they any closer to a real arrest in the murder?"

"They wouldn't say so if they were. It would be too embarrassing, after arresting Jacoby."

"Right. Does Dino know he's out?"

"I don't know, but Dino always knows everything."

"Call him anyway."

"Okay."

"And thanks, Herb, for taking this on. I'm tied down out here for a few more days." He looked at the bed, where what was tying him down was still asleep.

"Don't let her tie you up," Herbie said, then hung up.

Stone's phone rang again. "Hello?"

"It's Eggers. Our meeting is at ten AM, in the bridal suite."

"Is anybody getting married?"

"Actually, it's the Sierra Suite. I keep forgetting."

"I'll be there at nine-thirty. There's something I need to talk to you about before the meeting."

"Okay."

Stone hung up and got back into bed with Lara. She snuggled. Stone dozed off. Then the phone was waking him up again: eight o'clock. "Yes?"

"I have Arlene Summers for Lara Parks," a young man's voice said.

"Ah, she's in the pool, I think; can I have her call you back in ten minutes?"

He gave Stone the number. "Don't be late," he said. "Arlene has a meeting."

Stone hung up and gave Lara a shake. No sign of consciousness. He bent close to her ear. "Arlene Summers is on the phone."

Lara sat bolt upright, her eyes wide open.

Stone handed her the phone. "Call her right now. I told her you were in the pool." He handed her the pad with the number.

Lara stood up, dialed the number, and paced. "It's

Lara Parks for Arlene Summers," she said into the phone. "And good morning to you. Yes, I was in the pool. Very refreshing. Ten o'clock is perfect. Yes, I know the building. See you then." She hung up. "That was Arlene Summers," she said. "I actually spoke to her."

"I know. Maybe you should get a shower while I order breakfast." He ordered, then took the Baxter contract from her handbag, went down to the study and copied it, then went back upstairs and returned it to her purse. He could hear the hair dryer in the bathroom.

She came out of the bathroom naked. "I have an appointment with Arlene Summers at ten," she said.

"You told me when you were still asleep," Stone said. "Now, put on a robe for the butler. Breakfast is on the way."

At nine-fifteen, Stone was in a business suit; so was Lara. "You look perfect," he said to her. "I've got a meeting next door, but there's a car downstairs waiting for you. Be on time."

"I will, I will." She went back to applying her makeup. "I'm wearing the Ralph Lauren suit you bought me yesterday."

"Break a leg," Stone said and left the house. He walked over to the hotel and rode up in the elevator to the Sierra Suite.

Eggers was having coffee in a comfortable chair. "Have a seat, Stone. Coffee?"

"I just had mine," Stone said. He sat down and handed the Baxter contract to Bill, who read it quickly.

"This is awful," he said.

"Don't worry, that's not her signature on it. It's her autograph." He explained the difference.

"What do you want to do about it?"

"I want our L.A. office to scare the living shit out of him, and I want this to get the attention of the bar association's ethics committee."

"I'll fax this to our office. We'll file against him; no warning. And I'll get our ethics department on it right away." He picked up the phone and got started. By the time the meeting began, he was done.

Remembering why he was at this meeting, Stone concentrated on staring at their opponent, Edgar Wheelis, without blinking. Soon Wheelis was mopping his face with a handkerchief.

Eggers showed everybody out.

An attorney from the Woodman & Weld L.A. office arrived with a letter to the bar association from Eggers, who signed it and gave Stone a copy of Lara's lawsuit. "Get her to sign this, and we'll file it this morning."

"She's seeing a new agent right now, but I'll have her signature before the day is out."

Stone was back at his house at eleven-thirty, and his phone was ringing again. "Hello?"

"Listen, Barrington, this is Guy Baxter. I'm—"

"Ah, Mr. Baxter, what a coincidence! I was just signing my letter to the bar association about you and reading our lawsuit against you, which will be filed before the day is out."

"What? What are you talking about?"

"You clearly haven't read either of my two letters faxed to you yesterday," Stone said. "This might be a good time to peruse them." He hung up.

Baxter called again. "Now, listen, I'm sure we can work this out amicably," he said. "Just make me a decent offer."

"You want money for drawing up a fraudulent contract? You want to add extortion to your sins? We have no interest in settling this—how did you put it? 'Amicably'? It would be so much more fun to sue you and get you tossed off the bar. And when word gets around about the lawsuit, half of Hollywood will be in court to watch the fun, not a few of them witnesses against you, I expect."

Baxter was making choking noises.

"Oh, and by the way, Lara is meeting with Arlene Summers right now. Isn't that nice?"

"You'll never hear from me again," Baxter sobbed.

"Send me back the original of her autograph and an abject written apology. I want it inside an hour." Stone hung up.

18

Stone and Lara were sitting down to dinner at Spago, Beverly Hills, Wolfgang Puck's restaurant. Lara had returned to the hotel with a contract with Arlene Summers's firm. Stone had read it and had her sign it.

Wolfgang Puck came over and greeted them, and Stone introduced Lara as Arlene Summers's new client and Centurion's new leading lady. Then, over Wolfgang's shoulder, Stone saw a thickset man in flashy clothes coming toward them. He looked at Lara questioningly.

"That's Baxter," she said.

Wolfgang had moved on to the next table. Stone stood up. "I'm Guy Baxter," the man said confidently, flashing a lot of dental work.

Stone wrapped his dinner napkin around his right hand, a move that Baxter did not miss. "Go away," Stone said.

Baxter glanced at Wolfgang Puck, who had seen him coming. "Sorry to disturb you," he said, turning on his heel. Wolfgang followed him into the bar, had a few words with him, then returned.

"I'm sorry about that," he said to Stone and Lara.

"I've banned Guy Baxter from the restaurant, so he won't bother you again here."

"Thank you, Wolfgang," Stone said, and the chef went back to his rounds.

"I can't believe that you solved the Baxter problem and found me a new agent, all in the same day," Lara said, squeezing his hand.

"My law partner, Bill Eggers, got the legal work done, and Peter recommended you to the agent. I'm glad it went well."

From the direction of the front of the restaurant there came the noise of a loud crash. "Why do I think that has something to do with Baxter?" Stone asked.

"I wouldn't be surprised," Lara replied.

"Excuse me a moment," Stone said rising. He walked across the garden, through the bar and outside. Baxter was standing in the street, shouting at another driver, whose car had struck his elderly Mercedes. Stone turned and went back inside.

"It was Baxter's car," he said to Lara. They could see the reflection of flashing lights through the front windows. "I expect the police will be handling it shortly," Stone said. "Mr. Baxter is having a very bad day."

"It couldn't happen to a nicer guy," Lara remarked.

Back at the Arrington, they were getting ready for bed when Stone's phone rang. "Hello?"

"Stone, it's Art Jacoby. I can't thank you enough for your help today."

"Art," Stone said, "if you jump bail, I'll hire a bounty hunter."

"Don't worry about that. I'm getting a loan on my house, and you'll have your money back tomorrow."

"That would be a relief. What happened, Art?"

"Little Debby has suddenly decided that I'm the chief suspect."

"Does she suspect your girlfriend, too?"

"Not yet."

"I think you should both move temporarily."

"I'll think about that."

"Keep me posted on the progress." Stone hung up and turned his attention to Lara.

Dino woke him up the following morning. Stone picked up the phone. "Why is it that no one in New York can figure out what time it is in L.A.?"

"I never give it a thought," Dino said. "What time is it out there?"

"Four o'clock tomorrow morning," Stone replied.

"Oh, shut up. You want the news, or what?"

"Or what, I guess."

"The charges against Art Jacoby have been dropped, so you'll get your bail money back."

"Dino, that *was* worth being woken up in the middle of the night. Thank you."

"They probably haven't even cashed your check yet."

"That's a nice thought. I'll tell Joan to go get it. What caused Little Debby to back down?"

"The word is, somebody in D.C. had a word with her: bad press, and all that. I don't get the D.C. papers, but I'll bet the story is all over them."

"Good. She deserves it."

"In my book, she deserves worse. Having somebody arrested out of spite is a big leap over the line."

"It is." Stone's phone rang. "I've got a call coming in. Anything else?"

"You're half a million bucks richer again. Ain't that enough?"

"Bye, Dino." He pressed the incoming call button. "Yes?"

"Stone, it's Art Jacoby."

"I heard, Art. Congratulations!"

"Thanks, but the news isn't all good. As I was being released this morning, a cop I know called and told me that my girlfriend had been found dead in my house."

"Oh, Jesus, Art. I'm so sorry."

"When I got there, they wouldn't even let me go inside, but the detective on the case told me that she was shot."

"I don't know what to say."

"Neither do I," Art said. "I'm going to find a hotel I can afford and get some sleep. Jail is a very noisy place."

"Let me know what develops," Stone said. "I suppose I don't have to tell you to watch your ass?"

"No." He hung up.

Stone had barely hung up when Herbie Fisher called. "You're off the hook," Herbie said.

"I heard."

"I've got your cashier's check. When I get back to the office I'll messenger it over to Joan, and she can have it canceled."

"Thanks, Herb. I just spoke to Art Jacoby, and he told me his girlfriend was murdered while he was in jail."

Herbie was silent. "I was about to say, 'at least he has an ironclad alibi,' but I stopped myself."

"You automatically think like a lawyer," Stone said.

"I don't suppose there's anything else I can do for Art," Herbie said, "but tell him to call me, if he thinks of something."

"I'll do that. Bye." Stone hung up.

Lara sat up in bed. "There sure is a lot of talking going on," she said. "What's happening?"

"It's best if you go back to sleep," Stone said, and she did.

19

Stone was asleep for another hour before the phone rang again. He sat up, and Lara was gone from the other side of the bed. "Hello?"

"The president for you," a woman said.

"Put her on."

"Good morning!" Holly said brightly.

"Good morning. You sound chipper, did something good happen?"

"Yes, somebody checked my schedule and found out that I have to deliver a speech tomorrow at UCLA. I called Joan to see where you were, and she told me you're already there."

"What a coincidence!" Stone looked up to see Lara coming out of the bathroom—naked, as usual. He held a finger to his lips. "How about that?"

"I'll be there in a couple of hours," she said. "How about a swim, et cetera."

"Certainly."

"I'll be next door, of course, in the presidential cottage, but we'll find a way to manage that."

"Yes, we will."

"See you for lunch?"

"Of course."

"Bye-bye."

"Bye." He hung up.

"You look funny," Lara said. "Who was that?"

"That," Stone said, "is classified. "I'm afraid you're going to have to move back to Santa Monica."

"Oh, shoot. And I was enjoying myself so!"

"I was enjoying yourself, too, but this can't be helped. This area is going to be off-limits in about an hour."

"Hmmm. Sounds like you'll be waltzing tonight."

"Don't jump to conclusions."

"I do that all the time. It works for me, usually."

"Not this time. There'll be a car here for you in half an hour. Why don't you take the afternoon and do some apartment shopping? After all, you can afford something nicer, now."

"What a good idea! Can I drop by later for a drink and a swim?"

"I'm afraid not."

"Oh, that's right. It's off-limits."

Stone shrugged. "Those are the breaks. Still, we've had a couple of pretty good days, haven't we?"

Lara started toward him, but he held up a hand. "The maid will be here any moment."

"Oh, yes, the sheets will need changing."

"The whole house has to be made ready for an arriving group this evening." A group of one, he thought, but what the hell?

"Got it," she said, tossing her suitcase on the bed and opening it. She began emptying drawers and stuffing things into the case, while Stone headed for the shower. When he came out, she was gone, but there was a note on the dressing table mirror, drawn in lipstick. *It's been fun!* it read. Stone found a box of tissues and went to work on it. He checked the dresser drawers and found a lacy bra in the top one. He stuffed it into the pocket of his robe and finished checking the room for remnants of Lara.

Clean, at last.

Stone's phone rang. "Yes?"

"I'll meet you in your pool in two minutes," Holly said. "Don't worry, I've ordered complete privacy." She hung up.

Stone got into a bathing suit and a robe, grabbed a towel, and went downstairs. He could see a man on the front steps, hands behind him, facing away from the house. Stone paused, then realized he wasn't going away. He opened the door.

"Good morning, Mr. Barrington," the Secret Service agent said.

"Good morning."

"Your guest is at the pool."

"Thank you." As he approached, he could see that the gate was closed, and one side of it was covered in canvas. He opened it and walked inside.

"Hello, sailor," a voice said from the other end of the pool. Her robe and swimsuit were on a chair. He walked around the pool, dropped his own things, and dove in, with an intense feeling of déjà vu. He swam toward her under the water, appreciating the view as he approached.

Holly grabbed him by the hair and pulled him to the surface. "Hi, there."

"Hi, yourself."

They enjoyed a long kiss, then more of each other.

They were back in their suits and robes before lunch was served at poolside.

"This is all working very well, so far," Holly said.

"Very smoothly, indeed," Stone agreed. "I guess you've learned the drill."

"I've *established* the drill," she replied. "I figured out what it should be and required them to conform to it. I very nearly had to send the head of the Secret Service into retirement, but Bill Wright, now his deputy, took him aside and explained things to him, and he's been quiet ever since. By the way, in New York, the 'drill' includes no Secret Service at your house, unless I'm actually there, then outside and in the garage only."

"I like it," Stone said, and he meant it.

"I rather thought you might. I've placed your house here off-limits to them, too, except for one man at the front door and another at the rear. There's a platoon available, of course, should circumstances require. And they get to see the pool only to inspect it before I use it."

"So, nobody's going to open the gate?"

"Nope."

Somebody opened the gate. "That's lunch," Stone said. "Ah."

The cart was wheeled around the pool, and a waiter set the table, placed the food, and opened a bottle of wine.

Stone noticed a bulge in the small of the man's back. Looked like a nine mm.

Soon they were alone to enjoy their lobster salad. "I'm afraid dinner tonight is out of the question," she said. "An impromptu visit from the Japanese president."

"Ah, well."

"I'm yours until four o'clock, though, and I'll do my best to make up for the lost time."

"You've already done that," Stone said.

"Then I'll start building credit for the future."

20

Holly snuck out of the house at four in the after-noon, and he slept for a couple of hours. He had dinner off a tray in his lap and watched TV. Lara's series came on, and he watched it for the first time. She was wonderful, he thought.

The butler had just cleared away his tray when his phone rang. "Hello?"

"It's Eggers. I'm done here. You about ready to head east, say, tomorrow?"

"Sure. Wheels up at nine."

"Will you be alone?"

Stone thought about that. "Undetermined," he said. "You'll find out when you're aboard."

"See you at eight-forty-five," Bill said, then hung up. Stone thought for a moment, then he called Lara.

"What a surprise!" she said.

"When do you start shooting Peter's film?" he asked.

"We start rehearsing, let's see, six days from now."

"How would you like to spend those days in New York with me?"

"What a good idea!"

"I'll send a car for you at seven-thirty tomorrow morning," he said, "and I'll meet you at the Burbank airport."

"That's just grand."

"Make a note: the tail number is November One, Two, Three Tango Foxtrot—N123 TF. You'll need that at the gate for access to the ramp. Wheels up at nine. That means be aboard at eight-forty-five."

"Got it. See you there."

"Oh, there'll be one other person aboard, besides the crew: my law partner, Bill Eggers. You'll like each other."

"Fine."

They hung up, and Stone arranged transportation for himself and Lara. Then called Faith and gave her her marching orders. He got a very good night's sleep.

They departed on time, and Eggers and Lara did most of the talking. The cockpit buzzed Stone's intercom. "Yes?"

"Dino for you on the satphone," Faith said.

Stone picked up the handset. "You got the time right for once," he said.

"I'm a timely guy. You hear about Art Jacoby's girlfriend?"

"Yes, I spoke to him yesterday."

"Now Art has disappeared."

"Define 'disappeared.'"

"Nobody that I know can find him."

"I think that was his plan, after what happened to his girl."

"Well, he did a damn good job of it."

"Have you looked down the hall?"

"In his office here?"

"It's worth a try, and it's not a long walk."

"I'll call you back." They both hung up.

After a few minutes Dino called back. "Art's in his office, appears to be working."

"Glad to be of help," Stone said. "Anything else I can do for you?"

"Dinner tonight?"

"There'll be a girl, name of Lara Parks."

"Good. Viv is back from wherever the hell she was. Patroon at seven?"

"You're on." They hung up again.

"Everything okay?" Lara asked.

"We're having dinner with my friends, Dino and Vivian Bacchetti at seven," he said.

"How will I be dressed?"

"I will be wearing a suit and necktie. You will have to figure out the rest."

"I'll see what I can do."

"I'm sure you'll do it very well."

Eggers interrupted. "We closed the deal with Edgar Wheelis," he said.

"Then I did my job."

"Yep. The good news is I can't think of a reason ever to meet with him again."

Stone thought he'd better call Joan; he tapped the number into the satphone.

"Yes, sir?"

"I'll be in later this afternoon, with a guest."

"I'll tell Helene to expunge all traces of any previous visitors."

"Good idea. Did you get the bail money back?"

"It's in the bank," she said. "Somebody called here asking for Art Jacoby. I did my 'who's that?' routine, and it seems to have worked."

"He's in New York. If he should call and need a bed, send him to a hotel, maybe the Lowell."

"Will do. You will rest undisturbed."

"Thank you, ma'am."

"You're very welcome, sir."

"Oh, and please book us a table for four at seven, at Patroon."

"Certainly." They both hung up.

Eggers moved across the aisle, so that he could work unimpeded, and opened his briefcase.

Lara moved next to Stone. "This is a lovely airplane," she said, taking his hand. "It's a Gulfstream, isn't it?"

"It is. A G-500."

"I saw the seating plan, and there are two beds in the back cabin, aren't there?" She squeezed his hand.

"I think we should wait until we're home to have that transaction. We wouldn't want to shock Bill Eggers."

"He doesn't look all that shockable."

"He's not, really, but he's a terrible gossip. I'd hear about it every time I visit the Woodman & Weld offices."

"Don't you work there?"

"I work mostly from my home office, but I go to the law offices for meetings and such."

"Well, I wouldn't want to damage your reputation."

"The gossip would likely *improve* my reputation, but I don't want to hear about it from the people at the main office."

"I'll try and contain myself until we get home, then. By the way, where is home?"

"It's in one square block of Manhattan townhouses, built around a garden, and it's called Turtle Bay."

"Why?"

"Because it's in an area that used to be a bay, before it got filled in and built on a long time ago."

"Is there a bed?"

"Oh, yes."

"Oh, good."

21

Fred met them at Teterboro in the Bentley. Eggers had his own car. Stone introduced Fred and Lara, and they drove into town and into the garage. Fred took the luggage upstairs, while Stone led Lara into his office.

Art Jacoby was sitting on the sofa in Stone's office. Stone introduced Lara to him. Joan came in, too, and Stone asked her to take Lara to the elevator. "I'll be up in a few minutes," he said to Lara. "You might, ah, unpack."

She squeezed his hand and left the room.

"I hear you disappeared for a while, Art," Stone said, taking a seat.

Art shrugged. "It seemed preferable to getting shot in the head," he said.

"Arguably."

"Then I came to New York. Nobody would look for me here. Joan found me a hotel uptown, but I wanted to speak to you first before I check in."

"Go right ahead," Stone replied.

"I know it's hardly necessary to mention this, but please don't tell anybody where I am."

"Dino and his people know you're here. You went to your office at One Police Plaza."

"I've sworn them to secrecy, too."

"I'm sorry about your girlfriend," Stone said.

"I'm afraid I underestimated Deborah Myers," he said. "After the charges were dropped, I thought she'd just let it go."

"Apparently not."

"If I'd been smarter, Deana would still be alive."

"Then why are you still alive? Debby must have known where to find you."

"She needed me at large, so that she could hang Deana's murder on me. Then probably have somebody shoot me in the head and fake a suicide."

"I ask you again: Why are you still alive?"

"Because a detective friend of mine caught the case. He was at my house when I arrived. I called Deana's brother and asked him to make the burial arrangements, then I threw some things into a bag and caught the train to New York. I left some things here, and I came by to collect them. Joan packed them up." He stood up. "I'd better get going, and check in to the Lowell."

Fred came into the room. "Anything else, Mr. Barrington?"

"Yes, Fred. Please drive Lieutenant Jacoby uptown to the Lowell Hotel, then you're done until seven o'clock."

Jacoby offered his hand. "Thanks for your help with the hotel."

"You'll impress the hotel staff by arriving in a chauffeured car," Stone said. "All you have to do after that is tip well." He walked Jacoby to the door. "Are you going to go to your office every day?"

"No, I'll just call in for my messages."

"Watch your ass," Stone said.

"I'll do that." Jacoby took his leave.

Stone spent a few minutes dealing with correspondence and messages, then took the elevator upstairs. He walked into the master bedroom to find Lara unpacked and undressed, sitting up in bed with a book from Stone's bookcase in her lap. She closed it and tossed it aside.

"Now," she said, patting the bed beside her.

Stone undressed and slid into bed. "I'm right here."

Patroon was packed, and more people waved at Stone, since the inaugural festivities. Lara saw somebody she knew and stopped for a moment, and Stone sat down in the booth with Dino. "Where's Viv?"

"Her flight was delayed. She's coming straight from the airport."

He nodded toward Lara. "New?"

"Yes, from L.A. Her name is Lara Parks. Peter has cast her in his new film."

"How are you going to square this with Holly?"

"Holly suggested a while back that we be loyal in our affections only when we're in the same city."

"Didn't I read that she was in L.A. yesterday?"

"Yes, and she stayed overnight. Their paths did not cross."

"You think that's really going to work?"

"It's working so far. We both dislike celibacy."

"So she's sleeping with somebody else?"

"I don't know, and that's the way she wants it. So don't bring it up, and I don't want to hear about it from Viv. Perhaps you could have a word with her about that."

"I will, but I can't make any promises about how she'll take it."

Lara came to the table, sat down, and was introduced to Dino.

A moment later, Viv entered the room and walked toward their table, her eyes fixed on Lara. She sat down and was introduced.

"So good to meet you, Lara," she said. "How did you and Stone meet?"

Lara trimmed the pool scene off the beginning of their story. "I've been cast in Peter's next film, and he invited my leading man and me to dinner at his house. Stone was there, too, and when he heard that I wanted to come to New York, he very kindly offered me a lift."

"Stone is such a generous guy," Viv said, smiling icily.

"We were chaperoned by Bill Eggers," Stone said. "We were in L.A. on business."

Dino whispered something in Viv's ear. "What would you like to drink, my dear?"

Stone had never heard Dino call her that.

"My usual martini," she replied. "Dearest."

Stone winced, but Lara did not seem to have twigged to what was going on.

The maître d' arrived with menus, and Stone breathed more easily while they studied them.

They ordered, then Lara spoke up. "When Stone and I met, I recognized him immediately from the *People* photograph of him waltzing with the president."

"That's happening all too often these days," Stone said. "I might have been better off if I hadn't known how to waltz."

"Stone," Viv said, "when did you learn to waltz?"

"My mother sent me to a dancing class when I was twelve. She thought it might make me less awkward with girls."

"Well," Viv said, "that certainly worked, didn't it?"

Everybody had a good laugh, and things went more smoothly after that. Viv and Lara actually got on very well, Stone observed.

22

The following morning, after Stone and Lara had had breakfast and each other, and while Lara was showering, Dino called.

"I'm amazed," Dino said.

"At what?"

"Viv actually liked Lara. And when I told her about yours and Holly's arrangement, she thought it was a sensible idea."

"I'm so glad that we—Lara, Holly, and I—have won Viv's approval."

"You damned well ought to be," Dino said. "Otherwise, Viv would make life hell for both of us."

"If it helps, you can tell her that, if I have to choose between her approval and the company of women, the choice would be very easy."

"I am certainly not going to tell her that," Dino said. "Just try and be happy that Viv is on board with your lifestyle."

"For how long?"

"For as long as she is, and not a minute later."

"I'll keep that in mind. Listen, Art Jacoby has checked into the Lowell, and he doesn't want anyone to know."

"Yeah, Art and I had that conversation."

"Do you think you can spare a man in plainclothes to watch his back?"

"Watch his back against what?"

"Stray bullets. It appears that Little Debby has plans for him, and not happy ones."

"He thinks that Little Debby had his girlfriend popped, and he's next?"

"I think that accurately describes his current frame of mind."

"Okay, I'll put somebody on him. Do you want him to know?"

"If he's any good at all, he'll figure it out. If he doesn't, I'll tell him next time I see him."

"Which will be when?"

"When he seeks me out again."

"I think you'd better let him know now," Dino said. "Otherwise, he might mistake my man for one of Debby's, and hostilities could break out."

"Good point; I'll let him know. What's your guy's name?"

"Let's see," Dino said, and Stone could hear the drumming of fingers, probably on Dino's desk. "Frank Capriani!"

"You don't have to shout."

"Get in here, Frank!"

"What, was he walking past your door?"

"Yeah. You got the name?"

"Frank Capriani."

"Very good. You should have been a parrot." Dino hung up.

Stone called Art Jacoby.

"Yes?"

"It's Stone."

"Good morning."

"Where are you now?"

"Getting dressed to go out. I've got a fitting for a suit."

"An NYPD detective is going to find you and follow you around."

"Why?"

"Because Dino doesn't want blood to be spilled on the pristine streets of his New York."

"That's very thoughtful of him. And you. I expect you arranged it."

"His name is Frank Capriani. If you get a chance, shake his hand."

"Right."

"And go out heeled."

"To my tailor's?"

"You'll need him to conceal that bulge under your arm."

"Good point. Okay, I've no objections to being followed around."

"Buy him a cup of coffee—strike that—a drink. And, at the end of the day, cross his palm with silver."

"How much silver?"

"A hundred, if you can afford it."

"I can."

"Have a nice day."

"I'm determined to do that." They hung up.

Lara had been dispatched to upper Madison Avenue in Fred's care when Joan walked into Stone's office. "Donald Clark to see you."

"Here? Again?"

"I'm afraid so. I can ward him off, if you want."

"Send him in, I'll do it myself."

Donald Clark entered the room as if he owned the place. "Good morning, Stone." He took the chair opposite Stone.

"Morning, Donald. What can I do for you?"

"You can make a phone call for me."

"To whom?"

"To Hol . . . the president."

"Do you have a sprained dialing finger, Donald?"

"It's difficult to get through to her. She's the president."

"Yes, I remember something about that."

"She's taken away my Secret Service detail."

"Why are you surprised by that?"

"Cabinet secretaries all get Secret Service protection."

"Donald, do I have to remind you that you are not a member of her cabinet?"

"Well, sort of."

"She withdrew your name from the confirmation process. You are aware of that."

"Still . . . my wife has been murdered, and I'm . . . feeling nervous about it."

"No one is going to murder her twice," Stone said.

"I know that, but what if I'm next?"

"Donald, it's my information that you're a very wealthy man—something on the order of half a billion dollars, I read in the paper."

"Money is not bulletproof," Clark said.

"Let me remind you of a conversation between Scarlett O'Hara and Rhett Butler, in *Gone With the Wind*," Stone said. "Scarlett says to Rhett, 'After all, Rhett, money can't buy happiness.' Rhett replies, 'Scarlett, money can *usually* buy happiness, and even when it can't, it can buy some truly remarkable substitutes.'"

"What does that have to do with me?" Clark asked, not getting it.

"Money is bulletproof, if you're willing to spend enough of it."

He took a card from a desk drawer and pushed it across the desk. "This is the number of Michael Freeman, who is chairman and CEO of a company called Strategic Services—the second-largest security outfit in the world. Call him, tell him I referred you, and he will design a security detail that will protect you at all times, twenty-four seven, anyplace in the world."

"What would that cost?"

Stone stood and offered his hand. "Whatever it costs," he said, "you can afford it."

"By the way, will you give me Art Jacoby's number?"

"I'll ask him to call you."

They shook hands and Clark left, with Freeman's card in his pocket.

23

Donald Clark made a call from his car. They were connected immediately.

"Did you find him?"

"Barrington wouldn't give me his number."

"Did Barrington say he was in New York?"

"No. Have you tried his office here?"

"I've left three messages, and he hasn't called back."

"I don't know what else to tell you. If I learn anything I'll call you."

"Do that." They both hung up.

Art got out of the elevator at the Lowell, and it was immediately obvious who the cop was in the lobby. He was dressed in a decent, if unpressed, suit, wore a fedora and thick-soled shoes. He walked over to the man. "Frank Capriani?"

"Who wants to know?" the man asked.

"I'm Art Jacoby."

"And I'm your ride for the day. The car's outside." It was clearly his personal car, a worn-looking Jeep Cherokee.

"I hadn't expected to be driven," Art said.

"I guess it's your lucky day," Frank replied. "Where we headed?"

"Lexington Avenue and Sixty-fourth Street, Leung's Tailoring, upstairs, east side of the street."

"I hear somebody wants to do you," Frank said.

"I think somebody wants to perforate my suit, with me in it."

"That's always a problem."

"Dino says it's your problem."

Frank sighed. "Dino is the source of *all* my problems." He pulled up in front of the shop and put down his sun visor, which had a large NYPD gold badge imprinted on it.

"That's kind of a tip-off, isn't it?" Art asked.

"Think of it as pest control," Frank said. "We don't want any shootouts on Lex, do we?"

"We do not." Art trotted up the stairs. His fitting was ready, and he stood as still as he could, as the tailor marked final alterations with a slim piece of soap. He came back downstairs and got into Frank's car.

"No suit?" Frank asked.

"Tomorrow."

"Where to?"

"Let's do shirts," Art said, giving him an address on East Fifty-seventh Street. He went into Turnbull & Asser and picked out some swatches, then returned to the car and got in.

"Okay," Frank said, "tell me how a cop can afford your wardrobe."

"I had a daddy who died and left me in pretty good shape."

"Some guys have all the luck," Frank said. "I had a daddy, ran a candy store. He left me a jar of jawbreakers."

"Well, at least nobody's trying to kill you," Art replied.

"You haven't met my ex-wife."

Art laughed and answered his ringing phone. "Jacoby."

"It's Stone."

"Good day to you."

"And to you. I just had a visit from Donald Clark, who is upset because the withdrawal of his confirmation caused him to lose his Secret Service protection."

"You're kidding," Art said.

"No, he actually wanted me to call the president and plead his case."

"He's nuts. Who does he want to be protected from?"

"You, I believe."

"Me? What's my motive?"

"He thinks you think he killed your girl, and you want revenge."

"He's nuts."

"Do you think he killed your girl?"

"No, I think Little Debby had it done. You think he could be in cahoots with her?"

"Given their history, I think that's not a bad guess."

"Well, as guesses go, that's plausible."

"Speaking of protection, do you feel safe with Frank Capriani?"

"Sure. He's ideal. We've just come from my tailor and my shirtmaker, and nobody's taken a shot at me yet."

"Long may it wave," Stone said. "Call me if anything terrible happens."

"Sure thing."

Stone heard a strange noise, followed by a thud and a grunt. "Stone?" Art said, sounding a little wobbly.

"Something wrong?"

"Somebody just put a round into Frank Capriani's head."

24

Stone listened hard. "Art, are you hit?"

"No, I'm cowering as far under the dashboard as I can get. Frank is a mess."

"Is the car parked?"

"Do you know Turnbull & Asser?"

"Yes."

"Outside the shop, parked illegally."

"Arm yourself while I call the cops."

"Okay, but hurry." Art tugged his pistol from his shoulder holster.

Stone called Dino.

"Bacchetti."

"It's Stone. Somebody just took a shot at Art Jacoby, outside Turnbull & Asser."

"Was he hit?"

"No, but Frank was. He sounds dead."

"Okay, you call 911, now, and I'll get a detective squad over there." He hung up.

Stone called 911, then he called Art Jacoby.

"I'm still alive," he said.

"If they were going for a second shot, it would already have happened," Stone said. "Stay in the car, though. A detective squad will be there shortly. They don't like cops getting shot."

"I hear sirens," Art said. "Now, feet running."

"Then hang up and talk to them. I'll be there as soon as I can." He hung up and buzzed Fred.

"Yes, sir?"

"In the car, now," Stone said. He retrieved a nine mm and a shoulder holster, then ran for the car.

"Park Avenue and Fifty-seventh," Stone said. "Go up Park, and stay off the cross streets." Traffic was moving pretty well, until they came to a halt at Fifty-fifth Street.

"I'm getting out here, Fred," Stone said. "Park somewhere, and I'll call when I need you." He slipped out of the car and jogged up Park Avenue and crossed the street at Fifty-seventh. There were uniforms everywhere, and they had the sidewalk closed.

Stone flashed his detective's badge, hopped over a sawhorse and hurried to the door of Turnbull & Asser. People were coming and going, and he reckoned they had Art inside. He held up his badge and made his way into the shop. Art was sitting in a chair, surrounded by detectives, with his necktie undone and blood on his left shoulder.

Stone knew the detective in charge, Richard Becker. "Hey, Rich," he said.

"You got a finger in this pie, Stone?"

He nodded toward Art. "He's a friend. Can I talk to him?"

"Yeah, I think we've pretty much wrung him out."

Stone went over and pulled up a footstool. "How you doing, Art?"

"Better than I should be."

"What size suit do you wear?"

"Forty-two long."

Stone stood up and looked around the shop, saw an employee he knew. "Felix?"

He came over. "Yes, Mr. Barrington?"

"Will you see if you can find this gentleman a blazer or tweed jacket, forty-two long?"

"I'll be right back."

Stone stood behind Art and helped him off with his jacket, then turned to Rich Becker. "You need this?"

Becker asked somebody for a large evidence bag, then went through the pockets and handed the contents to Art.

Felix walked up holding two jackets. "Try one of these," he said.

Art slipped into the blue blazer. "Feels good," he said.

"Looks like it was made for you," Felix said.

"Thank you, Felix, put it on my bill," Stone said.

Felix nodded and walked away.

Stone said to Rich, "Are you through with him?"

"Yeah, you can get him out of here."

Stone leaned in. "He's staying at the Lowell. If you can't find him, call me."

Rich nodded.

Stone got out his phone and called Fred. "Where are you?"

"About ten feet from where you got out," Fred replied.

"Be right there." Stone looked around for hostiles, then led Art to the car and put him inside. He opened the armrest and found a bottle of water. "Drink some of this," he said.

Art gulped down half the bottle. "That's better," he said.

"Home, Fred," Stone said. He turned to Art. "Okay, now tell me what happened, and don't leave anything out."

Art took a deep breath. "Frank met me at the Lowell and drove me over to Lex and Sixty-fourth, for a fitting with my tailor."

"Who's your tailor?"

"Sam Leung's nephew. Sam retired. Then Frank drove me to Turnbull's and waited while I ordered some shirts. I came out, got into the car, talked to you on the phone, and then everything exploded, including Frank's head."

"I saw the car. The shot was fired from the sidewalk through your window, missed you and caught Frank."

"From the sidewalk? That's pretty bold."

"It is."

"I know Frank had an ex-wife," Art said. "Any other family?"

"Dino will find out and make the calls. He's used to it. Art, think about when you were walking out of the shop and to the car. Replay it in your mind, and tell me who and what you saw."

Art closed his eyes. "I brushed past two women to get to the car; they were still walking when I got inside. Before I did, I saw a black van parked behind Frank's car; I don't know the make."

"Could you see anybody inside?"

"Sort of, but there were reflections in the window that made IDing anybody difficult."

"Could somebody have gotten out of the van on the curbside, taken the shot, then gotten back in?"

Art nodded. "Yes. That could have happened. Probably happened. I can't recall anybody else."

"Did you tell the police about that?"

"I did."

"You still got your piece?"

"No, the cops took it."

"Did you fire it?"

"No, there wasn't time."

"I'll get it back for you, and if they're slow, I'll loan you something."

"Stone, I didn't remember this until now, but as I got into Frank's car, I caught a glimpse in the door's rearview mirror of a man getting out. He was wearing a black windbreaker and a black baseball cap."

"Did you recognize him?"

"Not exactly, but something about him made me think of Donald Clark."

25

As they drove into Stone's garage, Dino's official SUV pulled in behind them. Stone took Dino and Art to his study, where he poured Art some bourbon and handed it to him. "I expect you need this."

"You're right," Art said, taking a swig.

"I'm feeling left out," Dino said, and Stone poured him a Scotch and himself a bourbon, then Art recited his story to Dino.

"The guy getting out of the black van looked like Donald Clark?" Dino asked.

"I didn't say that, exactly," Art replied, draining his glass, which was instantly refilled by Stone. "I said there was something about him that reminded me of Clark."

"Think about it," Dino said.

Art appeared to do so. "His build," he said finally. "Clark is a pretty husky guy; not a lot of fat."

"That's a start," Dino said. "Think about his face."

Art tried. "Clean-shaven, sort of a pudgy nose, like a potato, but not big."

"Eyebrows?"

"Eyebrows?" Art asked.

"Were they dark or gray or blond?"

"Dark, I think. Clark has graying hair, fairly thick, no balding, but this guy was wearing a baseball cap."

"Anything on the cap? Product name; team name?"

"Something. Wait a minute, it was a Yankees' cap, with the 'NY.'"

"Anything on the jacket? A second color? An emblem of some sort?"

Art put his right hand on his left breast. "Here," he said. "The Yankees' lettering again."

"I think it's pretty safe to say that the guy is a Yankees fan," Dino observed. "Anything in his hands? Either one?"

Art closed his eyes again. "Shiny object," he said. "Silver." He clapped his hands together. "Short-barreled pistol, like a snub-nosed .38. Chrome or nickel-plated. Kind of old-fashioned, not like the chunky ones you see a lot of today."

"Glasses? Sunglasses?"

Art shook his head. "No."

"You're doing very well, Art," Stone said. "How about the man behind the wheel?"

"There was a reflection in the glass," Art said. "But I think he was short."

"The reflection?"

"No, the guy. The upper rim of the steering wheel cut across his face. He was a little uphill from me. The van was taller than Frank's Cherokee."

"Hair color?" Stone asked.

"Dark, I think. Fairly long."

"Could it have been a woman?" Dino asked.

"Possibly. Fairly thin face."

"Skin color?"

"White, pale."

"Hands on the steering wheel?"

"Same color."

"Nail polish?"

"No, I don't think so."

"Any rings?"

Art thought about it. "Yes! Something chunky, here." He led up his third finger, left hand.

"Like a class ring?"

"Right. Gold color, red stone, I think."

"So it's a guy," Dino said. "A college graduate, no less. A woman wouldn't wear a class ring on her third finger, left hand. That's reserved for an engagement ring or a wedding band."

"Unless she's unmarried and not engaged," Stone pointed out.

"Women have hope," Dino replied. "Art, close your eyes again and think about the inside of the van. Was there a partition behind the driver's head, or was their light coming from behind from windows?"

"It was dark, maybe a partition."

"So, a service van, like a plumber or an electrician or a delivery van," Dino muttered.

"Something else," Art said. "Two things: there was an object on the dashboard, near the windshield."

"What sort of object?"

"A book," Art said.

"Like a novel?"

"No, like a notebook. It had a wire binder."

"Like a steno pad?"

"Yes, but smaller."

"Like the notebook cops keep in a pocket," Stone said.

"Could be. And there was something hanging on the rearview mirror."

"Handicap placard?" Dino asked.

"No, some sort of personal thing. Cube shaped."

"I used to have something like that on my first car," Dino said. "My girlfriend made it for me, knitted it or something."

"Dice?" Stone asked. "I used to see big dice hanging on rearview mirrors."

"That was it!" Dino said. "I remember, I asked her, 'Why dice?' She said she didn't know why. She had a girlfriend who made them for her boyfriend's car, so she just copied them."

"So, it sounds like a personal vehicle," Stone said. "Not a rental. Something the guy drove all the time. He wouldn't have his dice in a rental."

"Do you mind if I take a nap?" Art said. "I'm drowsy."

"Sure, take the sofa, Art. I don't think you ought to go back to the Lowell."

Art moved to the sofa, shucked off his new blazer, and stretched out.

Dino motioned for Stone to leave the room with him. In the living room, he sat down, and Stone joined him.

"What do you know about Donald Clark?" Dino asked.

Stone shrugged. "He is supposedly a successful businessman of some sort. I read in a magazine that he is worth half a billion dollars."

"Probably in the financial world," Dino said. "You don't make that kind of money manufacturing widgets."

"Holly selected him as her secretary of commerce, but she withdrew the nomination after the mess at the hotel, and the sex rumors."

"That I knew," Dino said. He picked up his cell phone and pressed a button. "It's Bacchetti," he said. "I want to know everything there is to know about a Donald Clark." He spelled it. "Yeah, that's the one. He was going to be secretary of commerce, until he got his dick caught in his zipper. E-mail me whatever you find." He hung up. "Let's start treating this guy like any other suspect," he said.

26

Dino got up. "I gotta run. What are you going to do with the guy on the sofa in your study?"

"I'll have to find him a new hotel."

"What's wrong with one of your guest rooms?"

"We'd have a Secret Service problem there. They'd have to do a major background check, and it would annoy them that he was a suspect in a murder for a few minutes."

"You and Holly could also trip over him on the way to bed."

Stone nodded. "There is that, too. And we don't need to expand the list of who knows about our arrangement. That way lies Page Six in the *Post* and *People* magazine.

"Everybody wants to get in the way of your getting laid," Dino said.

"It seems that way sometimes."

"Where's Lara?"

"Out shopping. Fred is going to meet her somewhere."

"What happens if—rather, when—Holly calls and says she's on the way to New York?"

"There are airlines between here and L.A."

"Suppose she doesn't want to go?"

"Then we'll crate her and ship her."

"Whaddaya mean, 'we'?" Dino left, and Stone went down to his office. He buzzed Joan, and she came in.

"Yes, boss?"

"Lieutenant Jacoby is asleep on the sofa in my study. He's had a bad experience, and we have to get him out of the Lowell and into somewhere else."

"When?"

"Half an hour ago."

"I'm on it." She went back to her office.

Stone's phone rang, and he glanced at the caller ID: encrypted. "Hello?"

"Hi, there," Holly said. "How's tricks?"

"Tricky."

"How tricky?"

"A dead cop outside Turnbull & Asser, and another asleep in my study that I have to get transported to a hotel, to keep him out of harm's way."

"Is there room for me in all that?"

"You don't want anything to do with all that, but there's room where it counts."

"I'm on my way."

"Hang on, let me clear the joint, or the Secret Service will go nuts."

"What time would you like me to arrive?"

"Do you want to dine in or out?"

"Would it cause too much of a fuss, if we went to P.J. Clarke's?"

"Yes, and so much so that I don't think your detail would allow it. We need something with the tables farther apart: How about Caravaggio?"

"That sounds lovely."

"Can you come directly there at eight? Your driver can take your luggage to the house."

"Sure."

"See you then."

Stone hung up, and Fred came into the room. "Ms. Parks is back, sir."

"She certainly is," Lara said, squeezing past him with her shopping bags.

"Stand by, Fred. We're going to need you."

"Yes, sir."

Stone kissed Lara and pointed her at the sofa. "Have a seat and excuse me for a moment."

She did so, and he walked into Joan's office.

"Yes, sir?"

"I need a one-way, first-class ticket to Los Angeles."

"*You* are flying the airlines?"

"Lara is. Seven or eight o'clock."

"Okay."

Stone went back to his office and sat down next to Lara. "Events have occurred," he said, "that require your relocation."

She blinked. "To where?"

"L.A., unless there's somewhere else you'd like to go."

"Well, if I'm being tossed out, I guess L.A. will do."

"There's big trouble: a dead cop and an attempt on another, who happens to be asleep in my study."

"I guess that rules out a tumble on the sofa in there," she said. "How about this one?"

"Too much traffic."

Joan buzzed him, and he picked up the phone on the coffee table. "Yes?"

"Seven-forty-five," she said, naming an airline.

"Print an e-ticket." He hung up. "You're on a flight to LAX at seven-forty-five." He glanced at his watch. "That means rush-hour traffic. You'd better pack right now."

She sighed, kissed him and left the room, taking her shopping bags with her.

He buzzed Fred. "Give Ms. Parks fifteen minutes, then go up for her bags; she's headed to JFK, for a seven-forty-five flight."

Joan came in. "I got Art into the Morgan, a little farther uptown."

"Good. Have the Lowell pack his things and send them up there. Tell them mum's the word."

"Here's Lara's e-ticket," she said, handing it to him.

"Oh, and book me a table for two at Caravaggio at eight; a quiet table. And tell them there'll be an unnamed VIP."

"Practically done."

"And get Helene upstairs as soon as Lara clears the place, and tell her to make it look like it never happened."

"Of course. Do I get to know who's coming?"

"Holly. Tell Helene to keep the Secret Service guys fed and happy."

"Right. Flowers?"

"It couldn't hurt. Yellow roses, two dozen. Use the big vase. And get Art a car in fifteen minutes."

"Done." She went back to her office.

Stone walked upstairs and into the study. Art Jacoby was sleeping like a child. Stone shook him. "Art, wake up!"

Art opened an eye.

"We're relocating you; time to go."

Art sat up and rubbed his eyes. "Where am I going?"

"To another hotel: the Morgan."

"I'll have to stop by the Lowell."

"No need. They're packing your things and sending them to the new place. It's just up Madison a bit."

Art stood up, put his jacket back on, and smoothed the fabric. "Nice," he said.

"You're welcome. Come on, Joan has a car ordered for you. Fred is otherwise occupied." He sent Art downstairs, then took the elevator to the master suite.

Lara was tucking lacy things from a shopping bag into her suitcase.

"Is your luggage going to hold everything?"

"I may have to sit on it to close it, but yes."

Fred knocked on the door. "The car is ready, Ms. Parks."

Stone helped her close and latch the suitcase, and Fred took it away.

"It's been more than fun," Lara said, giving him a wet kiss.

"It sure has," he said.

"Call me when you come to L.A."

"By then, you'll be a very big movie star and unavailable," Stone replied.

"I'll be sitting home alone every night."

Stone walked her down to the garage and tucked her into the Bentley. As he walked back to his office, he could hear Helene upstairs, vacuuming.

27

S tone was halfway through a drink when the first Secret Service agent entered the restaurant and walked the length of the room and back, looking exactly like a Secret Service agent. Half the room was twigged, and the conversation level dropped by that much.

Holly walked in, wearing a full-length cape with a hood that partly concealed her face, and the restaurant-goers leapt to their feet and gave her a round of applause. So much for discretion. Two agents took up places with good views of the suspect diners.

Stone held her chair, and seated her with her back to the room. "Forgive me for not kissing you, but we would have made the papers," she said, keeping the hood up.

"We're going to make the papers anyway." Stone sighed. "I'll bet there's already a mob outside the front door. You may as well give them a look at that gorgeous hair."

She did so, and the room went "Ahhhh."

"They're repositioning the cars," she said. "Maybe that will throw them off."

"I'll give the agents a suggestion: when we're ready to leave, I'll have Fred pull up with the Bentley, while the photogs are camped next to your cars down the street. The cars will catch up, but it will be too late for the shutterbugs."

"That could work," she said, "once."

"Then I'll just have to keep being inventive."

"Or come to Washington now and then."

"Do you really think it would be any better there?"

"Well . . . Camp David could work, if we take separate helicopters." She laughed.

"I'll put that escape at the top of the list."

Menus arrived and, at Holly's suggestion, Stone ordered for both of them.

"I'll gain ten pounds," she said.

"Just eat a third of it. We'll take the rest home, so we won't have to go out tomorrow evening."

"I'm afraid we've only got tonight," Holly said. "Big jam-up in the Oval the morning after, and I have to direct traffic."

"Tell me something that you can't tell me about," Stone said.

"I can't tell you about that."

"Of course not, that's the point."

"I'm a stickler for the rules. If I start leaking, it will become a trend."

"How are Ham, Ginny, and Daisy?" he asked, speaking of her father, her stepmother, and her dog. "Or are they off-limits?"

"They're not, as long as you don't ask me where they are."

"Where are they?"

"Visiting Ginny's folks in Virginia. Dammit, you tricked me!"

"You're easy."

"More than you know," she said. "Eat fast."

Sometime during the night he woke up, and Holly was crying. Not bawling, but he could tell.

He kissed at her tears. "We can do this," Stone said. "Let's just enjoy what we can. Dinner with you is better than a dozen with Dino."

"I hope I'm a better lover, too," she said, wiping her eyes with the corner of a sheet.

"You'll have to ask Viv about that. Is there anyone in the White House you can talk to? Anybody completely trustworthy?"

"There's my secretary, Anna, who came with me from State, but she's sixty-four and turns beet-red if I mention the word *sex*."

"Then there's just me," he said. "There's always the encrypted telephone."

"Oh, I meant to tell you: the NSA tells me the Russians are trying to break in to that."

"Swell. Do we know when?"

"The Russians never rest."

"Go back to sleep," he said, cuddling her.

———

She was up before dawn. He could hear her singing tunelessly in the shower, then he dozed off, only to be awakened by the hair dryer.

She came and sat on the bed. "I'm going to appoint a special committee at the National Security Council to come up with a list of secure places we can make love."

"How about my place in Maine? There's nobody there in the winter."

"That would entail flying Air Force One to Boston, then boarding a U.S. Navy cruiser to somewhere off Southwest Harbor, then a Navy SEALs assault boat to your dock."

"I'll think again," he said.

"You keep doing that." She gave him a deep kiss and was gone.

He could hear the car doors slamming downstairs.

The bell on the dumbwaiter woke him again; breakfast was on its way up. Helene had not gotten the word; it was for two. He sent one back downstairs and took the other to the bed. He switched on the TV and the morning news showed Holly and Sam Meriwether walking past the Rose Garden and into the Oval Office, as if she had never left Washington.

Dino called. "You're all over Page Six again," he said.

"We can't just have a quiet dinner in an Upper East Side restaurant anymore," Stone said.

"Next time, you should have the management take the patrons' cell phones as they enter."

"It wouldn't work," Stone said. "A dishwasher, or somebody, would call us in for the standard fifty bucks."

"I suppose you're right."

"You know where Holly wanted to have dinner? P.J. Clarke's. Can you imagine?"

"It would have been a zoo."

"Worse. Somebody at a nearby table would have recorded our conversation."

"Are you ever going to get used to this?"

"I doubt it," Stone said. "Moving a president around is a big transportation challenge, and somebody will always notice. Holly suggested Camp David, if we each had a helicopter."

Dino laughed. "You keep trying!" He hung up.

28

Stone was at his desk when Dino called a second time.

"What?"

"Interesting news," Dino replied.

"Uh-oh."

"Not *that* interesting. I ran Donald Clark through the system and his file was blocked, 'For reasons of national security.'"

"A file block for the once and never secretary of commerce?"

"The intelligence people wield a heavy hand," Dino replied.

"What a shame one of us doesn't know somebody in that world."

"Both of us do." Stone was a personal adviser to Lance Cabot, the director of intelligence. "You want me to call him, or do you want to do it?" Stone asked.

"Lance likes you better."

"Well, if you're going to whine about it," Stone said, "I'll call him."

"Let me know what he refuses to tell you." Dino hung up.

Stone called Lance Cabot on his secure cell phone and was connected immediately. "Good morning, Stone. I trust last evening was a pleasant one."

"You've been reading the trash news," Stone replied.

"A rich source of intelligence," Lance replied. "Whatever can I do for you?"

"You think that's why I called? So you can do something for me?"

"You never call for any other reason, Stone."

"Okay . . . Dino and I are taking a look into Donald Clark, and his personal file is blocked."

"Blocked by whom?"

"By you, probably."

"Why would I do a thing like that?" Lance asked, wounded.

"To annoy Dino and me?"

"While annoying you and Dino has its pleasures, it's not happening on this occasion."

"Then you can get us in?"

Lance began tapping computer keys. "Got a pencil?"

"I prefer ink."

"Whatever you like. This is a onetime pass code for the file. You may not both view it simultaneously."

"May one of us print it?"

"Certainly not. It's good for one hour." Lance read out a thirty-six-character code of numbers and symbols, and Stone read it back to him.

"Have fun!" Lance said, then hung up.

Stone rang Dino.

"Bacchetti."

"All right, I've got a onetime, one-person pass code to Clark's file, and we can't both view it simultaneously, so you'll have to come over here."

"Why over there? Why not over here?"

"Because here is where it works." Stone glanced at his watch. "The pass code expires in fifty-seven minutes, so shake your ass." He hung up and buzzed Joan.

"Yes, sir?"

"Please ask Helene to make lunch for Dino and me in"—he checked his watch again—"in sixty-four minutes."

"Your wish, et cetera, et cetera," Joan said, and hung up.

Dino arrived around thirty minutes later, pretending to pant. He pulled up a chair next to Stone's. "Let's go."

Stone buzzed Joan.

"Yes, sir?"

"Please come in here with your pad and take notes."

"On my way."

Stone laboriously tapped in the thirty-six-character code. An on-screen message appeared: You screwed up. Try once more, because that's all you get.

"I think Lance writes the error codes himself," Stone said.

"Try and get it right this time," Dino moaned.

Stone handed him the pad with the number. "Read it aloud to me." Joan came in and sat down, pad and pencil at the ready.

Dino slowly read out the pass code, with Stone repeating every character as he entered it. Another on-screen message appeared: You made it. You have twenty minutes to read the file.

The screen wiped, and a typed form filled the screen, along with an older photograph of Clark, in a Marine dress uniform, his cap too large and resting on his ears, looking very young.

Stone began reading the file aloud, while Joan took shorthand.

It was four pages long.

"Done," Stone said, twenty minutes later. The screen image of the file dissolved and melted away.

"Done here, too," Joan replied.

"Type that up for us, please. We'll be upstairs."

Fred entered the room. "Gentlemen, lunch is served."

"Those words always make me hungry," Dino said.

Later over coffee: "It's difficult to believe that the pudgy, bald guy we know was once a Marine," Dino said.

"A Marine trained for special operations," Stone said. "You know what I find most interesting about that?"

"What?"

"That Donald fired Expert with the Colt 1911 .45."

"And with every other firearm in the special ops repertoire," Dino replied.

"What bullet killed Art Jacoby's girlfriend?"

"A .45," Dino replied. "Anybody who could fire Expert with that weapon is damned good. I could never even hit the target with it."

"Well, you're pretty good with most guns," Stone said, "so that says something about Donald's skills."

"What do you mean, 'pretty good'?"

"Okay, more than pretty good."

"Damn straight."

"So, we have motive and means," Stone said. "But opportunity?"

"I left my office in a rush, and I didn't bring the file on the girlfriend's shooting, but you can bet your ass Donald Clark has a solid gold alibi."

"Can't you remember what his alibi was?"

"I've got it," Dino said. "He was dining with the D.C. chief of police."

"Little Debby," Stone said. "How convenient."

"Ain't it?" Dino said.

"I'll bet that with a little elbow grease we can punch holes in that story."

"I'll get somebody with elbows on it," Dino said, getting out his phone.

29

Stone picked up his own phone and called Art Jacoby.

"This is Jacoby."

"It's Stone. Are you settled in?"

"Very comfortably, thank you."

"Dino and I just accessed Donald Clark's file, which was blocked for national security reasons. That make any sense to you?"

"There must be something in his background that nobody wants you to know."

"There was something," Stone said. "He was in the Marines when he was younger, and he fired Expert with a Colt .45."

"Interesting," Art admitted. "I couldn't do that, and I'm a pretty good shot."

"That's not the point. Your girl was killed with a .45, right?"

"Right, but she was shot at close range, so anybody could have done it."

"I'm embarrassed to say I didn't think of that. Did they find the weapon?"

"I don't know, and I can't call anybody at my shop, because I'm hiding out."

"Would they give that information to Dino?"

"Probably. Just ask for the case officer."

"There's something else."

"What's that?"

"Clark's alibi is that he was having dinner with Little Debby."

"That's not just interesting, that's suspicious," Art said. "In fact, as far as I'm concerned, culpable. It's too convenient."

"So they were both in on it, then they used each other as an alibi?"

"That's my opinion," Art said. "If I were running the case, I'd be all over that."

"Who's the case officer?" Stone asked.

"I don't know, and I can hardly phone anybody down there and ask."

"I'll get Dino to find out who the case officer is. What do I do then?"

"Ask him if he's tried busting that alibi yet. If he hasn't, the case officer's probably in on it, too."

"Good idea."

"You know, if they can't break the alibi, I think I'll just kill Don Clark myself."

"I didn't hear that," Stone said.

"I SAID, IF—"

"I mean *I didn't hear it*," Stone said. "And if you repeat it, I won't hear it then, either."

"Oh. Yeah."

"I'll get Dino on it."

"Good. Let me know what he comes up with."

They hung up, and Stone turned to Dino. "As far as Art is concerned, Don's alibi being Little Debby means they're in it together. Can you call the DCPD and find out who the case officer is? Art can't do it without exposing himself."

"If he does that in my city, he'll get arrested!" Dino said.

"You know that's not what I meant."

"Okay, you want me just to call down there blind and ask who the case officer is?"

"I was hoping that, being as well-connected as you are with all things police, you might know somebody who could find out without tipping our hand."

"I didn't know we had a hand," Dino said.

Stone sighed. "Nevertheless."

"All right, suppose I can get the name. What do we do then?"

"Art says to ask the case officer if he's tried to break the alibi. If he hasn't, then he's in on the murder, too."

"That's a pretty big leap, isn't it?"

"Maybe not. Art knows those people."

"And he's going to tell that to a judge?"

"Look at it this way: if we accept Art's hunch, and the case officer isn't interested in breaking the alibi, then we'll know that the murderer is one of at least three people."

"One of them being the case officer, then Don and Debby?"

"That's his hunch."

"Even if we can't prove it?"

"At least, we'll know."

"If we accept Art's hunch."

"You're making this sound like a bad idea."

"Well, I haven't heard anything yet that makes it sound like a *good* idea."

"You and I have solved cases based on a hunch," Stone said.

"At least it was *our* hunch, not Arthur Jacoby's."

"We're not on the ground in D.C.," Stone pointed out. "Art is. At least, he was before he went into hiding."

"Look," Dino said. "If you and Art start poking around in a D.C. case, it could bounce back on us, make people think we know where Art is."

"We *do* know where he is," Stone said.

"But nobody knows we know that," Dino pointed out.

"Maybe we should just drop the idea of breaking the alibi," Stone said.

"That's the first good idea you've had all day."

"Well," Stone said, consulting his watch, "it's only two-thirty."

"I have to go back to work," Dino said, rising. "I can't spend any more time today doing D.C.'s job for them." Dino left.

Stone thought about who he might know who would

know who the case officer was. He asked Joan for the initial report on the killing, which somebody had sent him. Art's girlfriend's name was Deana Carlyle. He had a thought, and it was worth a try. He called the phone number on the report.

"Homicide," a gruff voice answered.

"Hi, this is Detective Benson with the NYPD."

"What can I do for you, Detective?"

"Who's the case officer on the Deana Carlyle killing?"

"That would be Dean Casey," the man said. "Hang on, I'll transfer you."

Stone hung up. Deana? Dean? Case Casey? This was nuts. His phone rang. "Yes?"

"Art Jacoby for you on one."

Stone punched the button. "Hey, Art."

"The case officer is Dean Casey."

"I heard. And your girlfriend's name was Deana Carlyle?"

"Right."

"Who's Dean Casey?"

"Little Debby's most favorite toady in the whole world."

"So, he's suspect number three?"

"In my book he is."

"Thanks." He called Dino and told him, and Dino laughed out loud.

30

Stone was in bed with a book when Holly called. "We scrambled?" she asked.

"We are," Stone replied. "How was your day?"

"No worse than it should have been. This early in a new administration, everybody works hard to get it right, to prove their competence and my good judgment in hiring them."

"That's an astute observation."

"Thank you, I needed that. When you're at the top, everybody wants to praise your efforts, whether you deserve it or not."

"Another astute observation. They're piling up. You should keep a diary, and you can publish it when you're done."

"Can you suggest a title?"

"How about *Astute Observations*?"

She laughed. "Too self-congratulatory."

"Well, *somebody*'s got to congratulate you."

"You're doing just fine," she said. "What, if anything, happened to you today?"

"Well, the suspect list for the death of Art Jacoby's girlfriend has grown to three."

"And who are they?"

"Donald Clark, Debby Myers, and a cop named Dean Casey, all suspected of being in cahoots."

"Who's Casey?"

"The case officer, oddly enough. And, rumor has it, he's Little Debby's favorite toady. She put him in charge of the investigation."

"Well, that's very cozy, isn't it?"

"Any suggestions on how to proceed?"

"Is the girlfriend a federal employee?"

"I don't know what she does—ah, did."

"If she was, then killing her is a federal crime, and I can sic the FBI on them."

"I'll find out. Can you hang on a moment?"

"You're putting your president on hold? That isn't done."

"Only for a moment." He called Art Jacoby.

"Yes?"

"It's Stone. What kind of work did your girlfriend do?"

"She was a secretary at Justice."

"Thanks." Stone switched back to Holly

"You there?"

"Just barely. In all my time in this office, I've never been treated that way."

"Awwww. Good news, though. Art's girlfriend was a secretary at the DOJ."

"I'll goose the Bureau, then."

"Can you have the goose get in touch with me? I'll bring him up to date, off the record."

"I suppose I can suggest that." She sighed. "I miss you."

"You mean, you miss the sex?"

"That, too."

"As long as you don't miss only the sex."

Holly sang a few bars of "All of You."

"That's sweet!"

"You say that as though you're surprised I can be sweet."

"I've never doubted it."

"But you think of me, more, as tart."

"No, I don't think of you as a tart, except in bed."

"A lady in the parlor and a tart in the bedroom, huh?"

"Not the reference I would choose, but not inapt."

"Good," she said. "Now I have to go goose the Bureau. Expect a call."

Stone hung up and tried to settle back into his book, but thoughts of Holly kept intruding. His phone rang.

"May I speak to Stone Barrington, please?" A woman's voice, a very pleasant one.

"This is he."

"This is Maren Gustav; I'm a special agent of the Federal Bureau of Investigation."

Stone hadn't expected a woman; he hoped that didn't make him a misogynist. Probably not, he decided. "Good evening."

"You didn't expect a woman, did you?"

"I had no expectations of any kind."

"I believe we have a mutual acquaintance, who lives in a large house in Washington."

"I believe we must."

"May I take you to lunch tomorrow," she asked, "so we can discuss the matter?"

"That sounds good, but I'm in New York," Stone replied.

"What a coincidence, so am I!"

"Then when and where shall we meet?"

"At the Grill, at twelve-thirty?"

"Very good. How will I recognize you?"

"You can't miss me. I'll be wearing a badge, a helmet, and SWAT body armor."

"I'm sure the other patrons will find that entertaining."

"I'll know you from the waltzing photos in *People*."

"Oh, no."

"Until then." She hung up. Stone knew from past experience that it was unwise to form mental pictures of a woman, based only on her voice, but his bet was that she was not short, fat, and unattractive.

31

The following morning Stone had the thought of inviting Dino to join them at lunch but decided against it, until he had made his own assessment of Maren Gustav. He idled through the morning, then walked up to the Seagram Building and into the Grill's street-level entrance. He walked up the stairs into the bar, and the maître d' approached. "Ms. Gustav is waiting for you on the back row," he said, nodding toward the rows of table.

Her face was hidden behind a menu as he approached. "Ms. Gustav?" he said, and the menu went to half-staff, revealing a Swedish blonde who, sitting down, appeared to be quite tall.

"Ah, Mr. Barrington," she said, shaking hands. It was a hand with long fingers.

Stone sat down. "Please call me Stone," he said.

"And I'm Maren."

"As Swedish names go, isn't there usually a 'son' on the end of a Gustav?"

"There was, but I found it inconveniently long, and I got tired of spelling it for people."

"Perfectly understandable."

"Let's order, then we can talk."

The waiter poured him a glass of champagne, and he ordered the Dover sole.

"Make that two," she said to the waiter, "and we'll stick with the champagne." She handed her menu back and turned toward Stone. "Now, please tell me everything you know about the Deana Carlyle case."

"Actually, Ms. Carlyle's corpse is the second in line, after Patricia Clark's."

"Ah, yes. I've read that file, too."

"I believe the two murders are part of the same case," Stone said. He picked his way through the story, trying not to leave anything out. By the time he had finished, a Dover sole was staring back at him from his plate.

"Let's eat, then we'll talk more about the case," Maren said. They did so, and she pressed him for his personal history. He gave her the two-minute bio, instead of the sixty-second summary.

"Now, you," he said.

"I was born in a lovely house in the Stockholm archipelago of Sweden."

"Did the Bureau give you a hard time about not being a born citizen?"

"No, the house belonged to my grandparents. My parents had emigrated to the States years before, but my grandmother felt her grandchild should be born in her house, and not in a New York railroad apartment, which was where my parents lived at the time. They registered my birth at the American embassy, so there would be no nationality problems. I grew up on the Upper West Side, went to Columbia for my BA and my JD, and was recruited by the Bureau out of law school. That was more years ago than I am willing to admit. You look as though you're thinking about something else."

"I'm sorry. There are one or two things that may not be in the two case files you read," Stone said.

"Now, that's the sort of stuff I like to hear."

"Right. Here goes: Donald Clark has had threesomes with Deana Carlyle and Deborah Myers."

Her eyebrows shot up. "This case is going to be more fun than I thought."

"You ain't heard nothin' yet," Stone replied.

"Then do go on."

"Also Deana's boyfriend, Art Jacoby, a homicide lieutenant with the DCPD, was the unwarranted first suspect in the case. That position, as you can see, is now up for grabs."

"Heavens to Betsy," she said, fanning herself with her hands.

"*And,*" Stone continued, "Dean Casey, who is now supervising, is said to be Debby Myers's favorite toady. Art Jacoby feels that that makes Little Debby, as many like to call her, a suspect."

"Where is Agatha Christie when we need her?" Maren asked.

"You," Stone said, "are now the Agatha Christie in this case, and good luck to you."

They walked out of the building together, where a black SUV awaited her.

"May I give you a lift?" Maren asked.

"Tell me, how does a special agent rate a car and driver?"

"I'm sorry, I thought I told you: I'm the deputy director for criminal investigations."

"It's not all that far," Stone said, "but you can drop me." He gave her his address.

"Tell me again," she said as they drove away, "how did you become involved in this case?"

"It was easy," Stone said. "I returned to my suite at the Hay-Adams after the inaugural address, and the body of Patricia Clark was waiting for me on the living room floor."

"So, you were suspect number one, then?"

"For only a few minutes. The police commissioner of New York and his wife were a few steps behind me. And when Deb Myers turned up, they were able to assure her that I had been with them at the time of the death—and also with our new president. We dropped her at the White House after the ceremony, then changed cars for the trip to the hotel."

"How did you come to know the New York police commissioner?"

"During my service with the NYPD, which I told you about, he and I were partners, working homicide."

"Well," Maren said, "that's the most ironclad alibi I've ever come across."

They pulled up at Stone's house.

"Very nice," she said, checking it out through the tinted window.

"May I offer you coffee?" he asked.

"You may. Then I can satisfy my curiosity."

Curiosity about what? he wondered. "Your driver can park the car off the street," he said, using his remote control to open the garage door.

"Pull in there, Terry," she said, and the driver did.

Stone took her inside and pointed down the hallway. "My home office is down there." Then he took her upstairs.

"I love this," she said, admiring the living room.

"And this is my study," Stone said, showing her in and settling her on the sofa facing the fireplace. He picked up a phone. "May I have coffee for two, please?" He hung up. "Would you like an after-lunch drink?" he asked.

"Just some club soda with ice," she replied. He poured it and sat down.

"Tell me about the rest of the house," she said.

"Well, as I said, my office is downstairs, my secretary's, too. Down there is a small gym and the kitchen, which faces the common garden around which all the houses in Turtle Bay are built. Upstairs, there are two floors of guest rooms and one more floor up is the master suite. I also own the house next door, where my staff live, and the two houses together give me a large garage, which you have just seen."

Fred came in with the coffee and Stone introduced the two. "Would your driver like some coffee, Maren? Or you can send him home, and Fred will deliver you to your hotel whenever you like."

"Fred," she said, "would you please tell my driver that he's finished for the day and can leave?"

"Yes, ma'am," Fred said, and left.

"Now I'll have that after-lunch drink: Grand Marnier, if you have it."

"I have it in abundance," Stone said, then poured them each one. "May I ask you the question you are most often asked?"

"Six feet, in my stocking feet," she replied. "It helps when the need arises to intimidate a special agent."

"I can imagine," Stone said. "What else may I do for you?"

She gave him a warm smile. "I'll give you a hint," she replied. "It's most easily accomplished from a kneeling position."

"Are you sure that's what you'd like?"

"Very much," she replied.

Stone got up and closed the door.

32

They had adjusted their clothing and were finishing their drinks when the doorbell rang. Stone picked up the phone. "Yes?"

"It's Dino."

Stone pressed a button and heard Dino enter the house. "It's Dino Bacchetti," he said to Maren.

"How does my lipstick look?" she asked.

"Perfect."

Dino knocked on the study door. "Come in!" Stone answered.

The door opened. "Why was the door closed?" he asked.

"There was a draft," Stone replied. "This is the FBI's deputy director for criminal investigations, Maren Gustav," he said. "She's taken over the Clark business."

Dino shook her hand and pulled up a chair. He looked at them oddly, as if something were amiss.

"We're having Grand Marnier," Stone said. "Can I get you something?"

Dino stood and walked to the bar. "I'll get myself a Scotch," he replied, then did so and returned to his seat.

"Well, Director," Dino said. "How did you come to be on this case?"

"Since one of the victims, Ms. Carlyle, was a federal employee, that makes this a federal case. The president personally asked me to take it over."

"I'm an admirer of the president's judgment," Dino said.

"Thank you."

"Welcome to the case. It will be nice having someone in charge who is not in the bag or an idiot."

Maren laughed. "Thank you again."

"Has Stone taken you through the case?"

"Let's say that we have left no Stone unturned," she replied.

Dino's eyes narrowed. "Have you an opinion of whom we should suspect?" he asked.

"I believe that there are at least two suspects, possibly more," Maren said. "And one abettor."

"Do you have enough for an arrest?" he asked.

"Not until we turn one of them."

"Who's your candidate for turning?"

"I think Little Debby is the stupidest, so let's start with her; I'll go see her on my return to Washington."

"And when will that be?"

"That remains to be seen."

"Is Viv in town?" Stone asked.

"She is," Dino replied.

"Maren, will you join the Bacchettis and me for dinner?"

"I'd love to. I'd like a little nap and to freshen up. May I do that here, instead of returning to my hotel?"

"Of course," Stone said. "Let me show you upstairs. Excuse me for a moment, Dino."

"Go right ahead."

Stone took her up in the elevator and led her to the master suite.

"This is lovely," she said. "I believe I owe you something." Her hand wandered to his zipper.

"You may repay after dinner," Stone said. "I shouldn't keep Dino waiting. There are arrests to be made in this city." He kissed her on the forehead and left her to it.

Dino was gazing into the fire, sipping his Scotch when Stone returned. "I booked us into Patroon, in your absence."

"Thank you."

"What the fuck was going on when I arrived? There was something in the air."

"There was no fucking going on," Stone replied firmly. "You're not happy, are you, unless you suspect someone of something."

"I'm usually right," Dino said. "I must say, the quality of management at the Bureau is improving."

"I can't argue with that."

"How do you find these women?"

"Holly sent this one."

"I guess she feels guilty about leaving you without sex."

"Nonsense. I asked her to goose the FBI to get moving on this, and she went right to the top. Maren happened to be in New York on other business."

"She sounds like she's planning to winter here."

"Okay with me."

"Am I keeping you from her side, so to speak?"

"You are not. She wants a nap, and I am content with your company, for the time being. Did you call Viv?"

"I did, and she approved our dinner plans."

They had settled into their booth at Patroon, where Maren had insisted that she be seated facing the door. "The gunfighter's seat," she had explained.

They had just placed their orders when Stone saw Maren's eyes dart toward the entrance. "Opposition?" he asked quietly. He half-expected her to produce a weapon.

"My boss likes to think so," she replied. "He thinks I want his job."

A tall, distinguished-looking man suddenly appeared at their tableside.

"Good evening, Maren," he said to her.

"Good evening, Director," she replied. "May I introduce my companions?"

"Mr. Barrington and Commissioner Bacchetti and I have met, but I'm not acquainted with your other lovely guest."

"This is Vivian Bacchetti," Maren replied.

"I should have guessed," he replied, shaking her hand. "You're with Strategic Services, are you not?"

"I am," Viv said.

"Please give my warm regards to Mike Freeman," he said.

"Certainly."

"If you'll all excuse me, my dinner guest is waiting." He half-turned, then stopped. "And, Maren," he said. "I don't want to see this on your expense account."

"Ms. Gustav is my guest," Stone said quickly.

"Good." He walked away from their table and took a seat at a table across the room, where an attractive woman awaited.

"Who's the female?" Viv asked Maren.

"Oh, that is Ms. Not-His-Wife," she replied. "I'm filing that as an arrow in my quiver."

Everybody laughed.

"And thank you for being courtly, Stone."

"Why? You didn't think you were paying, did you?"

"A pity," Maren replied. "I was going to put it on my expense account."

33

President Holly Barker had just finished her daily intelligence briefing in the Situation Room and had returned to the Oval Office, when her secretary rang.

"Yes?"

"Madam President, Mr. John Henry Shaker, the director of the FBI, is here to see you."

"Does he have an appointment?"

"No, ma'am."

"Then ask him to wait while I receive the St. Mary's girls' choir," she said. "And send them in immediately."

A Secret Service agent opened a door from the hallway, allowing entrance to twenty teenage girls in matching white robes, followed by a porter pushing an upright piano on wheels, their director nun, and another nun.

"Good morning, Madam President," the nun said.

"Good morning to you, sister, and to all of your girls."

"May we begin?"

"Please do."

The girls began singing "The Bells of St. Mary's," from the old Bing Crosby movie of that name, accompanied on piano by the other nun.

Holly walked over to the thick, soundproof door separating her from her secretary and opened it slightly, to let the sound flow outside to her waiting room and the waiting director, then she returned to her desk and settled in her chair for the concert, which lasted twenty minutes. At the end, Holly stood, applauded, and called out, "Encore, encore!"

The girls rendered a haunting version of "Ave Maria." Afterward Holly went and shook each of their hands, and those of the nuns, then the room was cleared. Holly went to her desk and busied herself signing a stack of correspondence. Finally, she rang for her secretary. "You may send in the director," she said.

John Henry Shaker, ramrod straight and Brooks Brothers suited, entered the room.

Holly did not stand or shake his hand, but waved him to a chair facing her desk.

"Good morning, Madam President," Shaker said, seeming barely able to speak the words.

"Director. What can I do for you?" She signed another letter or two, then looked up. "Well?"

"Do I now have your full attention?" Shaker asked, icily.

"More or less," Holly replied. "Must I ask you again?"

"First, I must object most strongly to the replacement of my FBI security detail by Secret Service agents."

"Oh? Why?"

"As I am sure you are aware, my security detail, and those of my predecessors, have always been special agents."

"Certainly, I'm aware."

"Then I must demand that my special agent detail be returned to their work."

"Demand?" Holly asked. "You come into this office making demands?"

"Ah, request, then."

"*Request* denied," she replied, fixing him with her gaze. "It had come to my attention that your bureau detail were spending most of their time delivering and picking up your dry cleaning, or sewing on your buttons, or making you sandwiches."

"Are you suggesting that accomplishing those tasks myself would be a better use of my time?"

"Perhaps," Holly replied, "considering how you spend your time at work. You seem to have a more pronounced penchant for investigating the appointees of former President Katharine Lee than you did when Republicans held the office."

"The FBI does not undertake investigations that are unfounded."

"Perhaps the Bureau does not, but you certainly do. How long do you have left in your ten-year term, Mr. Shaker?"

"Nine months," he muttered.

"Perhaps that time would be better spent securing your future in the private sector."

"I had expected to be reappointed," he said, haughtily.

"I assure you, sir, your expectations are unlikely to be met. Is there anything else on your mind? Unburden yourself."

"I object most strongly to you assigning cases to my deputies rather than making your requests through me."

"It's only because I trust them more than I do you," she replied.

This time, he affected to be shocked. "Have I done anything to deserve your distrust?"

"You've certainly done little to deserve my trust. In any case, it is a matter of historical record that you have little in the way of investigative experience on your record."

"My experience is more on the administrative side," he said.

"I'm sure your record is a triumph of administration," Holly said, "but when I want something investigated, I tend to look to an investigator, not a shuffler of papers."

"Yes, I saw one of your investigators at work last evening at dinner, in New York, with a man not her husband."

"Deputy Director Gustav had business with Mr. Barrington and Commissioner Bacchetti, and she found a social setting more conducive to her work than an interrogation room. Incidentally, she is unmarried. I understand, however—from a source not related to the deputy director—that you spent the evening in a very public place with a woman not *your* wife."

Shaker actually shook. "The lady you refer to," he said, "is a *friend* of my wife."

"And you somehow think that sounds better?"

"Are you implying . . ."

"Implying? I am stating a fact, something you are ill-acquainted with."

Shaker stood, still trembling. "Have you anything else to say to me?"

"Well, it's your meeting, but as long as you ask, I do. You are to return to your office, and henceforth, remain there, conducting no business more boisterous than giving tours of the building to troops of Boy Scouts, and issuing no orders to any employee of the Bureau, beyond your secretary. If, at any time, you choose to retire and draw your pension, you may consider your resignation already accepted. Good day."

John Henry Shaker remained, for just a moment, frozen, then gathered himself and marched out of the Oval.

Holly buzzed the head of her Secret Service detail.

"Yes, Madam President?"

"FBI Director John Henry Shaker is on his way out of the building. Please meet him at the door and collect his White House pass and his parking permit. Tell him it's on my orders."

"Yes, ma'am!"

34

Joan buzzed Stone. "The president for you, on line one."

Stone pressed the button. "Good day, Madam President."

"And to you," she replied warmly. "I understand you had a pleasant last evening."

Stone wondered which part of the evening she was referring to. "Yes, we all had a very good dinner."

"And a very good nightcap, too, I hope."

"Quite satisfactory," he replied, getting a little more uncomfortable.

"Oh, Stone," she said, "you must get over being almost as famous as I, since *People* published those photographs of us waltzing. I get reports."

"I'd like to think I'm over that."

"And did you find Maren Gustav good company?"

"Define 'good company.'"

"I don't need to do that, and you mustn't mind if I send you pleasing companionship now and then."

"I'll try to be more grateful," he said. "But I'm beginning to feel that you are rendering me an unnecessary service."

"Perhaps so. Nevertheless, it gives me pleasure to provide it, and eases my guilt about being here instead of there."

"Then we'll say no more about it."

"If you wish. By the way, you might ingratiate yourself even further if you whispered into her shell-like ear that she's very likely to be the next director."

"Is Shaker taking a hike?"

"Let's just say that I have pointed him toward the Appalachian Trail and kicked him in the ass. My guess is, his ego will require him to head that way. You'll see it in the papers when it happens. In the meantime, I have denied him the White House, and I'm thinking of ordering a major renovation of his office. I think a lot of chintz would look nice in the Hoover building."

"I'll look forward to hearing about that. How are you holding up down there?"

"Well, the conversation with Shaker lifted my spirits a bit, as did a visit to the Oval this morning from the choir of a Catholic girls' school."

"Next, no doubt, it will be the cast of *Hamilton*!"

"What a good idea! I could never afford the tickets on a mere president's salary."

"Next time you're in town, I know where to get seats for only the price of a small house."

"Oh, good. Uh-oh, I'm told the secretary of defense is waiting. We'll talk soon." She hung up.

———

Stone worked on for a few minutes, when there was a knock at the other door.

"Come in," he said.

Maren looked around the door. "Am I disturbing you?"

"More than you know," Stone said.

She came over to his desk. "Is it legal to kiss you in these surrounds?"

"Strictly speaking, yes, but Joan has very sensitive antennae and tends to walk in at such times. Bob, over there," he said, nodding toward the sleeping dog, "wouldn't mind a bit."

"I'll try to control myself. I'm off to speak with Arthur Jacoby and Donald Clark."

"Dinner tonight?"

"Oh, good, where?"

"I'll think of something."

"Well, I'd better repair to the Carlyle and exchange these clothes for others," she said. "Or someone might notice."

"Joan certainly would, and I'd never hear the end of it."

"After dinner, your place or mine? I need to select the appropriate wardrobe."

"Appropriate would be nothing at all, and I think we should come here. The director of the FBI might be noticed coming and going with a man at the Carlyle."

"That's deputy director," she said.

"Perhaps for the moment."

She perked up. "Have you heard something?"

"The breeze bears rumors," he replied. "I hear Shaker is being encouraged to vacate that space."

"From your lips to God's ears."

"Here at six-thirty?"

"Done," she said, and closed the door behind her.

Joan buzzed him. "That Donald Clark character is here again."

Stone ground his teeth for a moment. "Send him in, and disturb us after about three minutes."

Donald Clark strode into Stone's office, looking more athletic and self-confident than on his last visit. "Good morning, Stone!" he boomed, taking a seat, uninvited.

"Now what, Donald?" Stone asked, with no attempt to conceal his displeasure at the visit.

"I've been cleared of anything to do with the murder of Ms. Carlyle," he said.

"Oh, really? Did the DCPD post a notice?"

"The DCPD has closed the case," Clark said confidentially.

"How did you come to hear that?"

"I have ears here and there."

"Well, you'd better have them cleaned," Stone said. "The DCPD has simply closed the case without further recommendation."

"And that is as good as it can get," Clark said.

"Perhaps so, Donald, but it can get worse."

His face took on a wary look. "What do you mean by that?"

"Tell me, Donald, what did Ms. Carlyle do for a living?"

"I believe that she was a secretary."

"Where?"

"I don't know. Does it matter?"

"I fear it's going to matter a great deal."

"Stone, what do you know that I don't know?"

"Ms. Carlyle was a secretary at the Justice Department."

Clark's face went blank. "So?"

"So, she was a federal employee, and the DCPD does not investigate the murders of federal employees."

"That's okay with me," Clark replied.

"The FBI investigates the murders of federal employees."

Clark's face seemed to collapse. "The FBI?"

"Yes, and in this instance, the case is being personally dealt with by the deputy director for criminal investigations, a woman called Maren Gustav, who has a big reputation for her dogged pursuit of perpetrators."

"Dogged?"

"Do you possess a dog, Donald?"

"Yes, a Lab, much like yours."

"Does he ever tire of chasing a ball?"

Stone thought the man was going to burst into tears. "And I believe she has an appointment with you today. Better check your calendar."

Donald Clark got up and left.

35

C lark had been gone only a quarter of an hour when Joan buzzed. "Art Jacoby, on one."

Stone picked up the phone. "Yes, Art?"

"Stone, the feds have picked up Deana's case. DCPD is out of it."

"I heard," Stone replied. "That's good news for you, isn't it, Art?"

"Why?"

"Well, because you are innocent, are you not?"

"I am."

"Then the FBI has a better chance of proving that than does the DCPD, whose fearless leader wants you hanged at dawn, does she not?"

"She does," Art admitted.

"That means that Little Debby will have no influence on the investigation."

"Yes," Art replied, brightly.

"Do you have an appointment today with someone called Maren Gustav?"

"I do. Who is she?"

"She's the deputy director of the FBI for criminal investigations."

"Her boss, Shaker, hates me."

"Don't worry about it, Shaker hates everybody. Anyway, there are substantial rumors that he is on his way out, and other rumors that Gustav may replace him."

"Uh-oh, then she's going to be trying to make a name for herself."

"Art, she's already made a name for herself. That's why she's on the fast track for the job. She doesn't need your head mounted over her fireplace."

"She's due here in ten minutes," Art said. "What should I tell her?"

"The truth, Art. And if you've sprinkled a fib or two around in your earlier statements, now's the time to iron out the wrinkles. She can smell a lie the way my dog, Bob, can sniff out a sausage from two rooms away."

"I'll remember that," Art said.

"Remember, too, that her eventual goal is Donald Clark. She just needs you to pave the way."

"Right."

"Call me when you're done."

"All right."

They both hung up.

Stone was finishing a sandwich at his desk, three hours later, when Jacoby called again.

"How'd it go, Art?"

"My shirt is soaked clean through."

"Well, let's hope that she does not equate the smell of sweat with lying."

"I didn't lie. I told her the same things, over and over, as she slightly changed the questions. You've heard of a steel-trap mind? That woman has a mind like a bear trap, and I was the grizzly in question."

"She's done with you now, Art," Stone said. "It's Clark's turn in the bear trap, and I have a feeling he's going to have to gnaw off his own leg to get free of her."

"I have to go take a shower," Art said and hung up.

Maren Gustav was shown by a butler into a large, mahogany-paneled room, festooned with hunting trophies—meat, fish, and fowl. There were not, she noted, very many books in evidence, and those present were, mostly, sporting in nature.

Donald Clark stood respectfully, shook her hand, welcomed her, and offered her coffee, which she declined. He offered her the opposite end of the sofa on which he sat, but she accepted a freestanding chair, instead.

"I understand you have a few questions for me," he said.

"On the contrary, Mr. Clark," she replied, "I have a great many questions for you, and I wish to record your answers." She placed a small recorder on the coffee table. "Do you have any objections to being recorded?"

"Certainly not." He shrugged. "Why should I?"

She noted the time and began to ask rapid-fire questions about his schedule on the day of the Carlyle murder, his companions at different times, and his past relationship with the various other suspects and witnesses, never consulting notes. Two hours and ten minutes later, she noted, she abruptly changed tactics.

"Mr. Clark," she said, with a little smile, "can you enumerate for me the occasions on which you had sexual intercourse with Ms. Carlyle?"

Clark blinked. "I decline to address that question," he said, finally.

"How about the nature of such intercourse?"

Clark collected himself. "I decline to answer."

"How about the occasions on which one or more others were involved, and what persons participated in such intercourse? And their names, genders, and occupations?"

"Decline. I will not bring others into this matter."

As if propelled by some spring-loaded mechanism, a man in a pinstripe suit, carrying a briefcase, entered the room at a trot through a rear door, crying, "Stop! Stop! My client will answer no further questions!"

"Oh, really," Clark said. "I don't mind." This with patent insincerity.

"This interview is over," the lawyer said to Maren. "Kindly leave the premises at once."

"I take it you would prefer to have your client answer these questions before a grand jury," Maren said, rising and picking up, but not turning off, her recorder. "I can arrange that."

"Go, go!"

"A subpoena follows," Maren said, then departed, noting the time on her recorder before switching it off.

Stone received her in his study, and Fred took her small suitcase and makeup bag away.

"Good evening," Stone said, kissing her. "You look lovely!"

"Thank you," she said, sitting.

"A drink?"

"Of course. A very dry martini," she replied.

"Is there any other kind?" he asked, pouring one out of a premixed bottle from the freezer, frosting the glass immediately.

"Where are we dining?"

"At Rotisserie Georgette," he replied. "Specializing in roast fowl."

"Sounds lovely."

"How did your day go?"

"Better than I expected," she said. "Art Jacoby will make an excellent witness either for himself or against Donald Clark. I pretty much wrung him out, but he has his story straight now."

"What about Clark?"

"I got everything I expected from him, and when I brought up the subject of sex, an attorney, apparently mechanically operated, sprang from somewhere, shouting 'Stop!' I'll see his client before a grand jury, where he will, very likely, take the Fifth."

"Very likely."

"I'll tell you this, though. He's scared, and that's the way I like my suspects."

36

Stone had his houseguest for a couple of nights, then she folded her tent and readied herself for departure.

"When will I see you in Washington?" she asked.

Stone gulped. "I rarely visit Washington, and when I do my time there is fully occupied."

"Oh," she said, sounding disappointed. "I thought that might be over."

Stone kissed her, took her downstairs, and put her into her car.

"If your investigation brings you north again, please let me know."

"Perhaps," she said, then drove away.

That afternoon, Stone had a sandwich at his desk. Joan stuck her head around the door. "Put on CNN," she said.

Stone turned on the TV, which was already tuned to CNN. "According to a source at FBI headquarters, Director Shaker has never been happy serving under President Barker. Other sources say he would be unhappy serving under any woman. After leaving his resignation at the White House, handing it to a Marine guarding the doors, Mr. Shaker returned to the Bureau, packed his briefcase and a few boxes of books and personal items, and left for his country house in Virginia. There was no farewell speech to the men and women he left behind."

"Who is replacing him?" Stone shouted at the TV.

"His replacement, Maren Gustav, is a sixteen-year veteran of the Bureau who has served in a number of posts there, climbing the promotion ladder steadily, and has been a favorite of President Barker's since the president served as CIA director."

"Thank you very much!" Stone yelled, then switched off the TV. "Joan, are you still there?"

She opened the door a crack. "Yes, sir."

He handed her Maren's personal card. "Send two dozen yellow roses and a card saying 'Congratulations' to her home."

"Do you want to send Mr. Shaker a farewell bouquet?" Joan asked.

"Are you nuts?"

"I'm on it," she said, and closed the door.

Dino called. "You see it on TV?"

"I did. Well-deserved."

"What's that going to do for the investigation of the Carlyle girl's murder?"

"I think that, given her interviews on Monday, she's

fully invested in it, and now she's in a position to bring more agents into it."

"I hear she has a bear-trap mind."

"You hear correctly. Dinner?"

"P.J. Clarke's, at six-thirty?"

"Done. You book." He hung up.

Stone arrived on time at Clarke's, and the remnants of the five o'clock crowd were still at the bar. A Knob Creek on the rocks was set before him. And when the bartender moved away, Stone saw two photographs taped to the bourbon shelf of the bar: one was of Maren Gustav, in a low-cut evening gown; the other was of Stone waltzing with the new president.

Dino materialized at Stone's elbow, with a Scotch before him. "Nice, huh?" He said, nodding at the photos.

"Danny," Stone said to the bartender, "get rid of the one with me in it, will you?"

"Sorry, Stone," Danny replied. "Orders from the owner."

"Take it down, or I'll run amok."

"Speak to the owner."

"Danny, when was the last time the owner was in here?"

"I don't know, last year sometime."

"I'm going to stop coming here."

"You can't do that, Stone. We'll go broke!"

"Live with it," Dino said.

"Distract me from what I'm looking at," Stone said.

"Did you hear the news?"

"Not since lunchtime."

"The new FBI director's first official act was to call the U.S. attorney for the District of Columbia and ask him to form a grand jury to investigate Art's girlfriend's murder."

"She doesn't waste any time, does she?"

"Well, she hung out with you for a few days," Dino pointed out.

"And look what happened to her!"

"I guess Holly isn't the jealous type."

"I asked you to distract me."

"Okay. A girl is at home walking around naked. There's a knock at the door. 'Who is it?' she yells. 'The blind guy,' he yells back. "Okay, come on in.' The guy comes in and says, "Hey, nice tits! Where d'you want the blinds?"

Stone laughed in spite of himself.

37

Maren Gustav was finishing her first days as director when she got a phone call from Mark Bernstein, the U.S. attorney for the District of Columbia.

"Good morning, Mark," she said, breathless to know what had happened.

"Good morning, Maren," he replied. "It went off pretty much as we expected. He took the Fifth."

"Then the media will convict him before we can."

"There's always immunity," Mark said.

Maren thought about it. If they gave Clark immunity from prosecution, then he could not take the Fifth, since he would not be incriminating himself. If he still refused to testify he could be held in contempt and jailed until he relented. "I think so," Maren said.

"The question is, to whom do we make the proffer of immunity: Clark or Deborah Myers?"

"I suppose we do have a choice," Maren said. "What happens if they both decline the offer and refuse to testify?"

"I suppose they could hold hands in federal prison," Mark replied. "Or, perhaps, we could arrange some conjugal time for them."

Maren laughed. "They might find that too appealing."

"He's still in the jury room," Mark said. "What's your preference?"

"Let's offer Clark the immunity. We'll see if he's the tough Marine he likes to think he is."

"I'll go speak to his attorney." They both hung up.

Mark Bernstein had been a classmate of Clark's attorney, Jeff Goode, at Harvard Law, and they had never liked each other much. It gave Mark a little thrill to be able to convey this message. He held up five fingers and the questioning attorney announced a short break.

Jeff Goode had been waiting in an anteroom, since defense attorneys were not allowed in the jury room. Mark took a seat next to him at the table. "How goes it, Jeff?"

"That depends on whether you believe my client's testimony."

"I do believe him, when he says that answering truthfully might tend to incriminate him."

"So, where do we stand?"

"We're offering immunity," Mark replied.

"Complete and total immunity?"

"Not for every misdeed in his miserable life; just for his actions with regard to his wife's and Deana Carlyle's murders, whatever they might have been."

"So, you've chosen to go after Little Debby, have you?"

"That remains an option," Mark said. "I'd rather convict her on the testimony of your client. You ought to be able to sell him that: he walks, and Little Debby doesn't. What could be nicer?"

"In Donald's eyes, it would be better if they both walked."

"We both know that's not going to happen," Mark said.

"Okay, I'll give it a whirl. Have the bailiff bring him in here, and don't rush us."

"Fine, take your time." Mark opened a door and summoned the bailiff. "Good luck," he said to Goode, and left the room.

Jeff Goode stood and shook his client's hand. "How's it going in there, Donald?"

"Pretty much as you said it would."

"You know the press is going to tear you apart, don't you?"

"What has to be has to be."

"There's always a way out, Donald, if you're willing to pay the price."

"What way? What price?"

"They're going to offer you immunity for two murders—your wife's and Deana Carlyle's," Goode said.

"To testify against Deborah?"

"To tell the truth. Which of the following two headlines would you rather see tomorrow morning? 'CLARK

LAWYERS UP, TAKES THE FIFTH ON MURDER CHARGE AND IS IMPRISONED FOR CONTEMPT,' or 'CLARK TESTIFIES AGAINST MURDERER AND WALKS FREE'? Those are the options."

"What will they do with me, if I just refuse to testify?"

"The judge will jail you, until you relent."

"For how long?"

"How long have you got to live?"

Clark blanched. "I don't like the sound of that."

"There's another possible headline you should consider," Goode said.

"What's that?"

"'CHIEF MYERS ACCEPTS IMMUNITY AND TESTIFIES AGAINST CLARK.'"

"She'd never do that to me."

"You never know," Goode said. "A year in federal lockup can soften the stiffest spines."

"I could appeal, couldn't I?"

"You'd lose."

"It's that definite?"

"It's cut-and-dried. One of you is going to get a deal, and the other is going to prison. You've been given the first shot at deciding that it's not going to be you."

Clark stared at the wall and said nothing.

"What's it going to be, Donald?"

"I need some time to think," Clark replied.

"I can ask them to break for lunch. That'll give you an hour, maybe an hour and a half."

"Can I call Debby?"

"No. You'll just have to sit in this room and think. I'll bring you a sandwich."

"Ham and cheese on rye, mustard, Diet Coke."

"I'll phone it in," Goode said, rising. He left the room, and Mark Bernstein was leaning on the wall outside.

"What's it going to be?" Mark asked.

"I gave it my best shot. Apparently, he doesn't like making decisions on an empty stomach."

"I'll call lunch."

"And I'll get him a ham on rye with mustard," Goode said. They went their separate ways.

Clark had been sitting alone for half an hour. He knew he was going to cave, and that annoyed him. He heard the door open behind him and turned to look that way.

An elderly black woman, pushing a cart of cleaning tools and supplies entered. "Cleaning lady . . . You mind?" she asked.

"Go ahead," Clark replied and turned away from her.

A moment later, he heard a ratcheting noise, one that he remembered from the firing ranges of his youth. He was about to speak, when something hammered into his head and he collapsed into a pool of his own blood and brains.

Another shot was fired into his head, then the door opened and closed again.

38

Stone was walking back from the Grill, after lunch with a client, when his phone rang. "Yes?" he said and continued walking.

"It's Dino. You want the latest news, or you want to see it on TV?"

"Dino, you know I hang on your every breath. What's going on?"

"Donald Clark got offed while in a grand jury hearing."

Stone was stunned. "While testifying? Who shot him, the prosecutor?"

"No, they were on a lunch break and Clark went to an adjoining room to meet with his attorney, who gave him the good news that the U.S. attorney was offering him immunity in the Carlyle case. He wanted to think it over, so the attorney left him alone while he ordered lunch."

"So, he got more than he ordered, and in the federal courthouse?"

"He got a .22 slug in the back of the head, and an extra one for insurance."

"Have we heard what Little Debby's alibi is?"

"Not yet, but I'll give ten-to-one odds that it will be a peach."

"I'm not taking that bet," Stone said.

"Anyway, an elderly black woman was seen in a nearby hallway, carrying a pail and a mop. You ever heard of Ma Barker?"

"A 1930s gang leader, wasn't she?"

"Right. Also, the sobriquet of a certain middle-aged black woman who works as a hit man—excuse me, hit lady."

"Is Ma Barker's alibi a peach?"

"You bet your ass it is. She was at choir practice at her church."

"Oh, that's good in so many ways!"

"You are right! She can put twelve ladies and a reverend on the stand to testify to her presence."

"Come on, nobody at a church choir practice would so blatantly lie for her."

"Right, but the cops have spoken to the twelve ladies and the reverend that she named—who were not, of course, necessarily at the church. You can bet they were well paid, though, and Ma Barker, too."

"That's breathtaking."

"Did I mention that the feds found a gray wig on fire in a trash can in the courthouse?"

"How about a weapon?"

"Nowhere in sight, and not in Ma Barker's house, either. They got a warrant."

"So everybody involved takes a walk?"

"Everybody but Donald Clark. He took a gurney to a slab downstairs."

"What's the old expression?"

"It couldn't happen to a nicer guy?"

"That's the one. My sentiments exactly."

"Are you going to tell Art Jacoby?" Dino asked.

"No, I thought you'd like to do that."

"No, I wouldn't."

"Well, I'm not going to tell him," Stone said. "Let's let him hear about it on the evening news. Talk to you later." He hung up. The phone rang again before he could get it back into his pocket. "Yes?"

"Stone, it's Art Jacoby; have you heard?"

"Yep."

"Donald Clark got himself shot in a federal courthouse."

"Art, I just gave you an affirmative response to your question."

"They suspect a black hit lady called Ma Barker."

"Art, you're not listening. I just heard it all from Dino."

"Why didn't you say so? Ma Barker is one slick lady," Art said.

"You know what her alibi is? Twelve members of her church choir and her Reverend."

"How do you know all this stuff? It just happened."

"Art, are you at home?"

"If you can call this hotel a home, yeah."

"Then sit down and compose yourself. Take a few deep breaths."

"I'm next on Little Debby's hit list. I'm not going to have any breath to spare."

"Art, I have to run now. Try and calm down. You'll live longer."

"Fat chance," Art said, then hung up.

Maren Gustav got a call from Mark Bernstein. She listened carefully, asked some questions, then hung up.

Her secretary came in. "Have you heard?"

Maren held up a hand. "I have heard, so you don't get to tell me the story."

"What are we going to do?"

"I don't know about you, but I'm going to think about it before I do anything. If anybody else calls, tell them I've already heard the news and, if it's a reporter, that I have no comment at this time."

"That's pretty ballsy," the woman said.

"It's the truth," Maren said, "all of it." She made shooing motions, and the woman went back to her desk. A moment later she buzzed Maren.

Maren picked up. "Was I not clear?"

"It's Stone Barrington, and he didn't ask if you've heard."

"Ah." She picked up the phone. "Yes, I've heard."

"I figured you had," Stone said. "I was calling for a different reason."

"Pray tell, what is that?"

"I hear that Little Debby's alibi was that she was in New York at the time of the killing. I thought that might necessitate a trip to our city by the nation's chief investigative officer."

"I like the way you think," she said.

"I like that you like the way I think. It will make your expense account look better if you just stay with me, rather than at the Carlyle."

"More good thinking." She looked at her watch. "I have a helicopter at my disposal, now, you know."

"I rather thought you did."

"I can be scratching on your door by six o'clock."

"I love that sound," Stone said. "What would you like to dine on?"

"You," she said.

"I hope your phone isn't tapped."

"Trust me, it's not."

"We'll dine in then."

"Oh, yes."

39

Maren Gustav's helicopter ran a little late, and Fred was announcing dinner as Stone greeted her. "Sorry, I got held up at the office," she said.

"You're just in time. Dinner's ready. Can you dine without a drink first?"

"I'm as hungry as a tigress," she said, as Stone seated her.

"I hope you like foie gras," he said.

"You can still get it in New York?"

"I expect them to ban it every time I think about it, so I try not to think about it."

Fred set two plates of perfectly seared foie gras before them, and they made all the right noises as they ate.

When they had finished the sauternes served with the first course, Fred came in with a platter and presented a thick porterhouse steak, then set it on the sideboard and carved it perfectly.

They made the correct sounds again, then finished their cabernet slowly.

"You were right about Little Debby's alibi," Maren said. "She's in New York."

"I'm sorry to hear that I was right," Stone replied.

"But do you know what she did before she left the federal building in D.C.?"

"I don't know. Used the ladies' room?"

"Do you know what else she did?"

"Pass."

"She took the elevator down to the basement."

"Shocking!" Stone said.

"Don't be a smart-ass. Do you know what's in the basement?"

"Cells?"

"A few holding cells, but what else?"

"The coffee machine?"

"The evidence locker."

Stone sipped his wine. "Locker?"

"Like, a big room, really, manned by one officer, who goes to lunch at the same time every day. Do you know what's in an evidence locker?"

"I'll take a stab. Evidence?"

"You're being a smart-ass again."

"Why don't you just tell me what she did?"

"She let herself into the locker, apparently with her own key, then went shopping."

"And what did she buy?"

"I should have said 'shoplifting.'"

"Then what did she lift?"

"At this point, it's all deduction," Maren said. "The evidence locker has lots of guns that are presumed to have been used in committing crimes."

"Ah, it all becomes clear," Stone said. "She wants an untraceable weapon."

"Or one that can't be traced further than the evidence locker."

"Where did you get all this information?"

"Secondhand from an informant who was in a holding cell, awaiting a court appearance, through a special agent who knows me. The evidence locker is not a room, exactly; it's a chain-link cage with long, open shelves."

"And your informant had a good view of all this?"

"He could see her through the chain link, facing him, and going through the firearms stash there."

"And she found something to her liking?"

Maren nodded. "What appeared to be a .22-caliber automatic with a silencer screwed on: an assassin's weapon, in short."

"I hope he took photographs," Stone said, "but I guess the inmates aren't allowed cameras."

"He managed to get his iPhone smuggled in by his girlfriend. He says he took half a dozen pics, and he wants to trade them for a kind word with the prosecutor about his suitability for a suspended sentence."

"What's he up for?"

"Burglary of a federal property. He'd normally get, maybe, five to seven years. He's not a first offender."

"So he wants to walk? Is it worth it?"

"To fry Little Debby's ass? Are you kidding?"

"So, when do we get to see the pictures?"

"After his sentencing."

"Not before?"

"That would be preferred, but he knows if he screws us we'll get him on something else."

"When's he being sentenced?"

"Tomorrow."

"Is the prosecutor on board?"

"He'd better be. The attorney general and I are tight."

"Does he know that?"

"It's being explained to him as we speak."

Dessert arrived, a crème brûlée, served with a small glass of Grand Marnier. Afterward, Fred poured them a cognac and retreated.

"Would you like another tour of the master suite?" Stone asked.

"I'd like a tour of the bed," she said.

They took their cognacs with them, and Stone conducted the tour personally.

40

Stone and Maren had sex, breakfast, sex, and a shower, in that order. As Stone walked out of his dressing room he heard Maren's phone ring in her dressing room. The conversation was short and loud.

She walked into the bedroom.

"They've moved our guy to a holding cell in the courthouse," she said. "He still won't give us the photographs of Little Debby in the evidence locker, until the judge hands him a suspended sentence."

"Can't you just confiscate his cell phone?"

"He passed it back to someone who will be in the courtroom. I can't search everybody. They'll all have cell phones."

"What was your decision?"

"I told the prosecutor to ask for a suspended sentence, and to sound good doing it."

"That's smart," Stone said.

"That's desperate."

"When do we hear?"

"I asked for his case to be called first, so not too long."

They had just walked into Stone's office when her phone rang. "Got 'em," she said and began scrolling through the shots. "No . . . no . . . no . . . NO! . . . YES!" She held the phone for Stone to see. "Only one good one, but look at it."

Stone took the phone and gazed at the photo. Little Debby, in person, holding a black semiautomatic pistol with about six inches of silencer screwed into the barrel. "Um . . ." he said.

"What?"

"Well . . ."

"Well, what?"

Stone turned the phone around and pointed. "Great shot of the gun, but you're missing most of Debby's face."

Maren snatched back the phone. "Holy shit! We only got her chin!"

"Great shot of the gun, though."

Maren moved back up the line of photos. "Here's a good one of her face," she said.

"Is it in the same frame as the gun?"

"No," Maren replied glumly. "You're a lawyer, will these photos stand up in court?"

"I'll give you a definitive answer: maybe. More important is how your witness's testimony stands up in court. If he can convincingly say, 'I took these photos, and they are all of Deborah Myers, including the one with the gun,' then maybe better than maybe. Of course, her attorney will be waving his arms and shouting 'Objection!'"

Maren's phone rang. "Yes? Hello, Mark. Yes, I got the pictures. Unfortunately not one of them includes both the gun and a recognizable shot of Debby's face. What's your witness's name? Eddie Craft? Good name for a burglar. Let me speak to him. I know he walked, Mark, but he must still be in the courtroom. He has to be processed. You mean he actually, physically walked out of the courtroom? Who processed him? Find him quick, Mark, and put him on the phone with me!" She hung up.

"Your side of that conversation did not sound satisfactory," Stone said.

"The judge handed down a suspended sentence, and a woman stepped forward and gave Mark the phone, then he gave it to the prosecutor. Then the judge said, 'You are free to go, Mr. Craft.' And he went."

"He would have to have been processed out, wouldn't he? I mean, courts don't function without paperwork."

"The judge told him he was free to go, and he didn't hesitate, he went. Nobody tried to stop him."

"Then I think what you need is a good, old-fashioned APB, an all-points bulletin, for Eddie Craft. You need to have a heart-to-heart with him, and sooner rather than later."

"I'm aware of that," she said, pressing a button on her phone. "Mark, issue an APB for Eddie Craft. Charge? I don't know, loitering. I need him back long enough to depose him and get his signature on his testimony. Right, and hurry!" She hung up. "Your suggestion has been taken."

"That makes me feel so happy," Stone said.

"You're being a smart-ass again."

"It's my nature."

"Of course," she said. "Well, I'm going shopping."

"The cure-all for anxiety of every variety," Stone said. "Don't worry, the Justice Department can reach you at Bloomingdale's."

"They'd better," Maren said. She gave him a wet kiss, then left.

Eddie got into the rear seat of a black Lincoln town car, right after Shelley Moss. "JFK international departures," she said to the driver.

"Which airline?" the driver asked.

"I'll let you know," she said, then turned to Eddie. "How long until the flight?"

He glanced at his watch. "Two and a half hours. We should already be there," Eddie said, nervously. "These days, it's at the gate three hours before the flight."

"Sweetie, we've got plenty of time at this hour." She opened her handbag. "Ticket and passport and everything in the safe."

"We can't walk that through departure," Eddie said.

Shelley dug into the bag and came up with a folded sheet of paper. "Sign this," she said.

Eddie read it. It was a customs declaration for the outgoing cash. He signed it.

"We'll get this stamped, then we're legal all the way," she said. "I'll take care of it at the airport."

"I bet you will." He laughed.

"A little cleavage goes a long way," she replied. "I packed your clothes; two bags and a briefcase are in the trunk. I don't travel quite that light. Some of my stuff is on the front passenger seat. Get ready to pay for overweight."

At the airport they got two carts, loaded them, then looked for the Virgin Atlantic check-in desk.

"Let's take the one with the male attendant," she said. "Upper Class."

The young man, entranced, did not charge them for the overweight.

The line was short, then they were in. "Now, over there," she said, toward a small sign that read U.S. CUSTOMS. "Stand by outside the door with the luggage, where they can see you. I'll go in." She undid another button on her blouse and strolled in.

Eddie could see her talking to the customs agent and showing him her document, among other things. He gazed at her approvingly, then stamped the document, and she returned. "We're all legal," she said. "Let's take a walk through security."

They took a look in her handbag, and she handed over the stamped document. A pat-down with the wand, a stroll through the metal detector, and they were through.

"An hour and a half to spare," Shelley said. She pointed at the duty-free shop. "Let's get a fifth of something."

An hour and a half later they were seated in Upper Class and taxiing. Eddie looked out the window and saw two NYPD cars, lights flashing, pull up to their gate, have a look around, then drive on.

"I think we're going to make it," Eddie said.

"You bet your sweet ass," Shelley replied.

41

Eddie Craft and Shelley Moss got off the flight at Heathrow and made their way through the nothing-to-declare customs exit without being stopped. Through the swinging doors was a line of drivers holding up cards bearing their passengers' names. Eddie steered them to one with the card reading *Schwartzkopf*, and soon, they were in the rear seat of an elderly Bentley.

"Who's this guy we're staying with?" Shelley asked.

"Alfie Bing," Eddie said. "Wife's name is Edie. Alfie is a very great, old-time thief of anything that isn't nailed down. He lives off Belgrave Square."

"That's a pretty tony neighborhood, isn't it?"

"Alfie's a pretty tony burglar. This is his Bentley. He bought the ass-end of a long lease on a big flat twenty years ago, and he's still got a couple of decades to go."

The Bentley pulled into a mews and drew up at a garage door. A uniformed butler stood in a doorway beside the garage. He directed them upstairs, while he and the chauffeur dealt with the luggage.

"Wow!" Shelley said as they entered a heavily decorated drawing room. "I've never seen so much stuff in one room!"

"Alfie has a steel-trap mind and a memory like an elephant," Eddie said. "He's got every piece in this room cataloged in his head. He can tell you who he stole it from and its present-day value."

"Doesn't he worry about being raided by the cops?"

"When he got out of prison after a two-year hitch, twenty years ago, Alfie disappeared into this flat, under a new name, Bing. He didn't leave these rooms for more than a year. He had a colleague steal his court and prison files—all on paper in those days, so he might as well have vanished into thin air. He started wearing a toupee, too, and grew a moustache."

A short, thin man in an excellent toupee, a handsome moustache, and a well-tailored suit entered the room and threw himself into Eddie's arms. His wife, Edie, tall and beautiful, joined them and introductions were made. Shelley thought his toupee undetectable.

"How long can you be with us, Eddie?" Alfie asked.

"I think a few weeks will do it, if that's all right."

"Not long enough. How bad do they want you?"

"Not bad enough to come looking here. They don't have a charge, really." He told Alfie the story. "They didn't even have time to assign me to a parole officer."

"You're good, then. We've got a nice little suite of rooms for you, one floor up."

———

Stone, Maren, Dino, and Viv sat in the dining room at the Carlyle hotel, sipping drinks while their dinner was prepared.

"What's the latest on Eddie?" Dino asked.

"He seems to have vanished in a puff of smoke," Maren replied. "Somebody saw them get into a town car, so we figured an airport, but we've no idea which one."

"A computer search should have brought up their names and flights," Dino pointed out.

"Funny you should mention that," she said. "The computer system at JFK went down for a couple of hours and scrambled some files. We finally got them landing at Heathrow, London, but too late, and they haven't checked into any known hotel in the U.K."

"Staying with friends, no doubt," Stone said.

"There was one other thing," Maren said. "He filed a customs form, declaring two hundred thousand dollars in cash, outbound."

"Probably staying with somebody not known to the police," Viv remarked.

"Stands to reason," Maren said.

Alfie took them all to the Sailing Sloop, an old Chinese restaurant, and ordered at least a dozen dishes for the four of them.

Alfie looked around to see that no other diners were

close, then leaned in. "I've got an eye on a country house," he said.

"I can't imagine you living in a country house," Eddie replied. "You're not the type."

"Not to live in, dummy, to steal from."

"What's there?"

"Pictures, four of them."

"It's worth the time for just four? Isn't there a collection?"

"Oh, sure, and it's nice stuff, but these four pictures are by an American artist named Matilda . . . something. I've got it written down at home."

"And who's Matilda?"

"She's the best unknown painter you never heard of," Alfie said. "She had a few pictures in the Metropolitan Museum, and the gift shop there printed up postcards of four of the pictures, and they sold out, wham! They reprinted, and they kept selling out, and now she's one of the better-known artists in America, and the value of her work has increased by a factor of about forty, compared to what they were a few years ago."

"I know this must be a dumb question, Alfie," Eddie said, "but if she's so well known now, where are you going to unload them?"

"I've got a buyer in a Scottish castle all lined up. He's offering a quarter million apiece. Now, that's a low price compared to what they'd bring at auction, but think about it: it's a one-night, million-pound job!"

"That's attractive, I'll admit," Eddie said, trying not to salivate. "What's the security like?"

"Tough, but here's the thing. The same owner has a house in Wilton Crescent, and it's wired up with the same gear as the country house. I've been practicing on that. By the time we pull the job, I'll be slick on all the gear."

They finished dinner, and Alfie had the staff pack up all the leftovers, which were considerable. "Lunch, tomorrow," he said. "Maybe lunch for a couple or three days."

On the way home, Alfie had his driver swing down Wilton Crescent, driving slowly. "That's the house," he said, pointing out the window. "See the two lamps on? Looks like the owner is home, doesn't it?"

"How do you know he's not?"

"Because his airplane isn't parked where it would be if he were in the country."

"Where's that?"

"On the estate where the country house is. There's an old RAF station on the property that was used to fly intelligence missions into France during the Second World War. He's got a Gulfstream, and he flies it in there, and they send a fuel truck down from Southampton to fill it up for the trip back. I got a guy who can check the hangar every day, if I like, and we pick a night when the hangar is empty. Simple as that."

"Sounds like it," Eddie said. "But I want to see you get by the security in the London house, before I'll commit to the big job."

"How about tonight?" Alfie asked.

42

Eddie Craft followed Alfie Bing into a nondescript saloon car housed in his flat's garage. Alfie handed Eddie a zippered leather case. "Hang on to my tools," he said.

They drove the few streets to Wilton Crescent, where the lights in the window of the subject house still burned. Alfie drove past the house in question, then turned into a mews with an electric gate. He took a remote control from the tool kit, clicked it, and the gate's bar rose. "A gift from a mate who tends bar at the Grenadier pub at the end of the mews," he explained.

The mews, Wilton Row, was lit by a pair of dim street lamps, just enough light for a drunk to stagger home without stubbing his toe on a paving stone.

Eddie parked the car and led the way to a small door next to the garage. "When this opens," Alfie said, "I've got to run very fast to the control box on the landing. Your job is to quickly close the door when you're inside. Ready?"

Eddie nodded. "Right."

Alfie picked the lock, and the door opened. He ran as fast as he could up the stairs to the landing, while Eddie closed the door as instructed. Alfie opened the box and took out a coding device, fastening it to terminals in the control box with alligator clips. He turned on the instrument, and it began to search for a code at a very fast clip.

Eddie watched the numbers fly. "It's not finding it," he said.

"Patience, my son."

The device found a number, and Alfie tapped it in. "Okay, we're in. Follow me."

Eddie followed Alfie up the stairs, and they emerged into a darkened hallway. There was a night-light burning green near the floor, nothing else.

"You see?" Afie asked. "It works the same way, down at the house in Hampshire."

"Okay," Eddie said. "I'm sold."

They backtracked, reset the control box with the code, and left in Alfie's car.

"Now, I've got one final advantage to show you," Alfie said. "When we get home."

Stone and Maren had just collapsed into each other's arms when his cell phone rang.

"Don't get that," Maren said.

"It's a scrambled line," he said. "It only rings if it's important." He picked up the phone. "Yes?"

"Stone?" Familiar voice and accent.

"Felicity?"

"Yes, my darling."

Maren covered the phone with her hand. "Is that Felicity Devonshire?" she asked.

"Please be very quiet," Stone said. He got up and went into his dressing room. "How are you?"

"I'm very well, thank you, but I've just had a call from one of our security patrol cars in Belgravia."

"Oh?"

"Yes. The lamps in your front window are out."

"I'm sorry, I don't know what that means?"

"It's not a code word. It means that the two lamps in your front window, which should be burning, are not."

"Oh. Is that bad?"

"They are wired into the very excellent security system that we installed in your Wilton Crescent house. The only thing that will turn them off is entering the six-digit security code into one of the control boxes."

"I see."

"Not really," she said. "This is very worrying. I called to find out if you want me to send a team into the house."

"I guess," Stone said.

"Or, would you rather have your house looted?"

"Please, send in a team," Stone said.

"It shall be done. I'll call you back after breakfast." She hung up.

Right, he thought. Five-hour time difference.

"You come back here," Maren ordered.

Stone followed her instructions.

"Now, what are you doing receiving phone calls from the head of Britain's MI6 security service in the middle of the night?"

"It's not the middle of the night there," Stone said.

"Did I ever tell you what a jealous woman I am?" Maren asked, kittenishly.

"No reason to be concerned," Stone said. "The security system at my London house may have been breached."

"Why would that concern the head of MI6?"

"They installed the equipment, and they have instructions to call her if there is a breach."

"Is someone in the house?"

"I don't know. She's sending a team to find out, then she'll call me back after breakfast."

"Breakfast tomorrow?"

"No, they're five hours ahead of us."

"Oh, right."

She pulled him back onto the bed. "Let me see if I can make you forget all about that."

She did, until the phone rang again. Stone took it into the dressing room. "Yes?"

"The house had been entered, but nothing had been disturbed. The team compared it to the photographs they took a while back."

"Any explanation?"

"Yes, someone used a device that ran through all possible codes. They reset it two minutes later."

"Why would someone want to be in my house for two minutes?" Stone asked.

"That is known only to those who entered," she said. "Now, rejoin whoever is waiting for you."

"Thank you, Felicity. I'm grateful to you." But she had already hung up.

Stone was awakened by the bell on the dumbwaiter.

"Breakfast!" Maren sang out cheerfully.

"Yes, breakfast," Stone said.

"Why do you look worried?" she asked. "Didn't you sleep well?"

"Not very well," he said. "I kept waking up, wondering why someone would break into my house in London for two minutes and not take anything."

43

Stone was at his desk when Joan buzzed. "Dame Felicity Devonshire on one," she said.

Stone pressed the button. "Good morning again, Felicity, or rather, good afternoon."

"Good day, Stone. I had a thought about the reason for your break-in last night," she said.

"I'd like to hear it," Stone said. "It kept me awake."

"You have a virtually identical system, that my people installed in Windward Hall, do you not?"

"I do," Stone said.

"What if last night was a dry run for breaking into the Hall?"

Stone found the suggestion alarming. "I see."

"What, in particular, do you have in the house that would be of great value?"

"Define 'great value.'"

"Something that could be sold immediately for a lot of money."

"Well, I think I left a couple of wristwatches in the watch winder in my dressing room."

"Even greater value."

"There's wine that could be sold at auction."

"Too easy to trace. I mean, Christie's and Sotheby's advertise those sales and keep records."

"Well, I have a few of my mother's paintings. They've gone up in value in recent years. I know, because I buy them when I can. But they would be easily traceable, too."

"Not if the thief were working for an existing client who is an art lover, or a lover of your mother's work, in particular."

"You mean, someone who placed an order for the pictures?"

"And to enjoy them in his home or place of business. That's what I mean."

"Can you send a team in there to have a look around?"

"I'm afraid not. We've got something of a panic on that I can't go into, but it's all hands on deck, I'm afraid. Why don't you call your security provider?"

"I'm speaking to her, as we speak."

"Oh, yes, you are, aren't you? How about your caretaker, Major Bugg?"

"He's out for knee replacement surgery."

"Oh, dear."

"I suppose I could call Inspector Holmes, of the local constabulary."

"I'm afraid they are also participants in the panic," Felicity said.

"You think I should come over there?"

"That's what jet aeroplanes are for, isn't it? Coming over here?"

Stone thought about it.

"If we get our panic cleared up, I'll be down tomorrow afternoon."

A few days with Dame Felicity was an alluring notion. "I suppose I could pop over," he said.

"How lovely. Will you give me dinner tomorrow evening?"

The cook lived on the estate. "Of course."

"What time?"

"I'll call you from the air when I have a firm ETA," he replied.

"Shall I bring a toothbrush?" she asked, coyly.

"I can't imagine that you would need more than that," he said. "See you tomorrow evening."

"I'll go quell the panic," she said.

Eddie walked downstairs from his guest suite and rapped on the door to Alfie's study.

"Come!"

Eddie entered and found Alfie sitting at his desk. Next to that was something covered with a cashmere throw.

"Good morning, Eddie," Alfie said cheerfully. "I trust you slept well."

"I did."

"I wanted to show you this last night, but I was knackered." He handed Eddie some postcards. "These are the pictures we wish to, ah, borrow from Windward Hall."

"From where?"

"Windward Hall is the name of the country house. In this country, they are always given names by their owners or their ancestors."

"Gotcha." Eddie riffled through the postcards. "Very nice," he said. "I don't know much about art, except how to steal it, but I'd buy these myself."

Alfie stood up, took hold of the cashmere throw and pulled it away. It had covered four medium-sized oil paintings.

"Holy shit!" Eddie was amazed. "Did you already steal them?"

"Of course not," Alfie said. "These are forgeries."

Eddie took a closer look. "These look real to me," he said.

"That's because they *are* real. I have this guy who can copy anything, right down to the brushstroke. Not even a lot of experts can tell the difference."

"Well," Eddie said, "if he's so good, why don't you just give these to your Scottish guy and tell him they're the real thing?"

"Because he's smart enough to figure it out and mean enough to cut my throat—or have it done. He's not a bloke you want to mess about. I have a good working relationship with him, and I don't want to cock it up."

"You know best, Alfie."

"Thank you, my son."

"So, when do we do it?"

"Tomorrow night. I need to get my man to check out the hangar at Windward Hall."

"I'm game," Eddie said.

Maren knocked on Stone's office door and stuck her head in. "I'm off," she said.

Stone got up and went to her. "Is your work here done?"

"I got word that Little Debby is back in D.C., so that's where I need to be."

"Any luck nailing down Eddie Craft?"

"His name is on a list," she said. "I hope he turns up, because I could really use him in court."

"Well, I've got to go to England for a couple of days to look into this break-in. Felicity seems to think it was a rehearsal for a job on my house in the country, which has the same security system."

"You're lucky I'm not the jealous type," Maren said, "or I'd shoot down your airplane."

"Then, as you say, I'm lucky." They kissed and she went to her car, which was waiting in the garage.

Stone buzzed Joan. "Get Faith and everybody on board for a flight to England tomorrow, wheels up at seven AM."

"Ah, you have a dinner date tomorrow night, don't you?" Joan asked.

"Don't ask, just alert the cook."

44

S tone was taxiing the Gulfstream from Jet Aviation at Teterboro to Runway One, with the Bacchettis in the passenger compartment, when his cell phone rang. "Yes?"

"Where are you?" Holly asked.

"Taxiing for takeoff," Stone said, "on the way to England for a few days. Dino and Viv managed to get some time off, as they usually do, so they're aboard."

"A pity. I'm coming to New York. What, or who, takes you to England?"

"A security breach at my London house. The country house is probably next. I suspect a burglar at work."

"What did he take from the London house?"

"Nothing, apparently. It seems to have been a dry run for Windward Hall, since they have identical security systems."

"Will you see Felicity?"

"Her service is in some sort of panic; she may be down to Hampshire, if she sorts it out."

"I'm jealous."

"Oh, good!"

"Beast!"

The tower called: "N123 TF, cleared for takeoff."

"I've been cleared for takeoff," Stone said, checking for traffic, then turning left onto the runway. "Bye-bye." He centered the tiller and moved the throttles forward. Soon, he was climbing, then turning northeast. He switched on the autopilot, got out of the left seat, and was replaced by Faith, his regular pilot. He went aft, settled into a seat opposite the Bacchettis, and the flight attendant brought them freshly squeezed orange juice.

"Mimosa, anyone?" she asked.

Dino opened his mouth, but Viv beat him to it. "Too early for you," she said.

"Hair of the dog," Dino replied.

"Nonsense," Viv said, then opened her copy of the *Times*. "How long, Stone?"

"Around six hours. We've got a big tailwind."

"I love a tailwind," Viv said.

"Who doesn't?"

Dino filched the business section of the newspaper from his wife.

"You never used to read the business section," Stone said.

"I never used to have money," Dino replied. His late father-in-law had left him comfortably fixed, annoying his ex-wife to no end. "Now, I enjoy watching the market."

"Will we see Felicity?" Viv asked.

"She has some sort of flap on at work, but if she can

resolve that, yes. I'll call her when we're an hour or so out and find out if she's in London or Beaulieu, at her house there."

"I think I can guess where she'll be," Viv said. "After all, she is motivated to fix her flap, with you on the way. Does Holly know where you're headed?"

"She called as we were taxiing," Stone said. "She knows all."

"Or suspects," Viv said.

"Viv, my darling," Dino said. "Shut up."

"I'm just . . ."

"I believe the word you're looking for is 'prying.'"

Viv made a disgusted noise and disappeared behind her newspaper.

As the sun set, Stone picked up the satphone and dialed a number.

"Ah, just as you said you would," she said.

"Just as I said."

"And your ETA?"

"Seven o'clock, your time, give or take."

"I'll wait for you in the library," she said. "What would you like me to wear?"

"Something that will impress Viv Bacchetti. She and Dino are along."

"I will be delighted to see them," she said.

Stone could not detect any irony. "They'll be delighted to see you, too. You and Viv can bring yourselves up to date on the international gossip, and Dino and I can listen quietly."

"Sounds perfect. I'll see you seven-thirtyish."

In London, Alfie Bing got a call. "Hullo, boss," a voice said.

"And to you," Alfie replied. "What say you?"

"It was just starting to get dark when I visited, and the hangar was unoccupied."

"Very good," Alfie said, then hung up and turned to Eddie Craft. "We're on," he said. "We'll leave around eleven; it's an hour-and-a-half drive, that time of the evening."

"I'm at your disposal," Eddie said. "Are we going heeled?"

"I never do," Alfie said. "I prefer my wits to carrying a gun. I'm much less likely to get shot, even if the opposition is armed. I do take along a cosh, though. A rap behind the ear can do much to discourage interference."

"I take your point, but do you mind if I carry?"

"I do mind. If you wish to do so, find your own jobs."

"I yield to your authority," Eddie said.

"And I'll pat you down to be sure you're good," Alfie replied.

Stone and Dino changed into their dinner suits and went down to greet Dame Felicity, while Viv took her time.

"Viv apologizes," Dino said, after kisses had been exchanged.

"No need," Felicity replied. "She's a woman, after all, and we must always look perfect for you lot."

"So *that's* why it takes so long."

"View it as a compliment."

"I will, unless I'm hungry," Dino said.

"You look lovely," Stone contributed. "I love the dress." The butler came round with a silver tray, bearing their drinks. "May I prepare something for Mrs. Bacchetti?" he asked Dino.

"She'd like a very dry martini with two anchovy-stuffed olives the instant she sits down," Dino said. "She gets surly if she has to wait for her martini."

"I shall be ready, Commissioner." He repaired to the butler's pantry.

"What is the condition of your flap?" Stone asked.

"What flap?" Felicity asked, blandly.

"The one that was defying solution, last time we spoke at any length."

"Oh, that. I simply assigned one of my deputies to handle it, then got into the car and drove down here, chasing the police car ahead of me."

"I'm so glad," Stone said, as Viv swept into the room.

They gave her a little round of applause, and by the time she sat down, her martini had materialized before her.

45

Alfie Bing drove Eddie Craft down to Hampshire, keeping the saloon car right at the speed limit. He had no desire to attract attention; one had to be careful of the little things.

He drove past the main gate to Windward Hall and saw the hangar in the distance. There appeared to be a light on inside. Alfie passed the hangar, made a U-turn, and stopped, he and Eddie staring silently at the building.

"That looks awfully like a jet aeroplane in the hangar," Alfie said, finally.

"It does, doesn't it?" Eddie said. "A long drive for nothing."

"Perhaps not," Alfie responded. He drove farther up the road, until the Hall itself came into view.

"Light on upstairs," Alfie said. "What's the time?"

"Half past midnight," Eddie replied. "Someone's likely getting laid."

———

Just beyond the lamp in the window, Stone and Felicity were getting laid. They performed slowly and artfully, as old friends will, each knowing what pleased the other. Then things heated up, until they made a point of climaxing together.

"That was just wonderful," Felicity said.

"I can't think of a better word," Stone replied. "I love the afterglow."

"Perhaps we would glow a bit better, if you switch off that lamp," she said.

Stone turned and pressed the button that turned off all the lights in the house still burning, except those in the guest room, which were managed by the occupants.

Ah, there," Alfie said. "They're abed." He pulled into the parking lot of the nearby pub, the Rose & Crown, shut off the car, and unscrewed the cap on a vacuum canister. "Coffee, Eddie, or will you kip for a bit?"

"I believe I'll nap," Eddie replied, and put his head back onto the seat.

"As you wish," Alfie said. "I believe I'll think this through while you kip."

Alfie had committed the house's plan to memory, and, in his mind, he watched Eddie and himself enter the building through the kitchen door. Then, using only a taped flashlight for a narrow beam, make their way, first to the control box for the alarm, then into the library, where the four Matilda Stones hung in their frames. After a bit, he dozed, too.

Eddie awoke first and checked his watch. "Alfie," he said, quietly. "It's just past two o'clock."

Alfie sat up straight and looked around. "No moon, no traffic, no lights in the house. Ideal." They both got out of the car and went to the trunk, where Alfie had black raincoats, watch caps, and cloth masks that would hang on their ears and cover everything but their eyes. "If we should encounter resistance," he said, "under no circumstances remove the masks. If someone gets close enough to reach for them, I'll use my cosh, and then I will decide whether to leave and, if so, what to take with us. Agreed?"

"Agreed," Eddie replied.

Alfie removed the canvas carryall that contained the forged paintings, closed the boot lid gently, and began walking up the road, on the opposite side of the house. "This is the last time we'll speak, until we're back in the car," he said. "If traffic appears, just lie down next to the road, and it will pass us by.

Eddie nodded and followed his leader.

Stone got up in the night and found the bathroom in the dark. He relieved himself and then returned to bed, trying not to wake up.

Alfie had made it over the estate wall with a big assist from Eddie, and they both dropped soundlessly onto the grass beyond. Alfe held up a hand to say *Be still*, and he listened for a minute or two for a dog, a footstep, or the cocking of a shotgun. He heard only an owl, from some distance.

Alfie knew that the estate's dog went home with a staffer, usually the retired Royal Marine, Major Bugg. And he was grateful for that. He had an air pistol in his pocket that fired a dart, but he was glad not to have to use it. The two men walked around the house, then slowly and silently up the steps to the kitchen door, where Alfie switched on his flashlight and examined the lock. Just what you'd expect on a country house kitchen door, he mused. He opened his zippered case and examined a selection of skeleton keys, choosing the largest one. Too big; wouldn't go in. He returned it to the case and chose the next largest. It slipped in perfectly. He retracted it and picked up a small can of WD-40 oil, then sprayed the inside of the lock. The key went back in, and the lock turned smoothly and noiselessly. Alfie wiped any stray oil from the lock, returned the key to its case, and put a hand on the doorknob, turning it very slowly. The door eased open.

Alfie motioned Eddie inside and made closing motions for the door, then he moved as quickly as possible to a closet on the other side of the kitchen, where the control box for the security system lay, expecting it to chirp at any moment, signaling an entry of the house. To his surprise, the opened box made no sound. He pulled Eddie close by the lapel and whispered into his ear, "They didn't arm the system. Piece of cake, now."

Alfie walked in a measured way down the hall toward the study, keeping close to the wall to minimize creaking floorboards. The study door was unlocked, as he had expected; he ushered Eddie into the room and slowly closed the door behind him. He took the carryall containing the forgeries, walked across the room, following the needle beam of the flashlight to where the paintings hung. He went over each with the flashlight to be sure they were what he wanted, then examined the frames, motioning Eddie to remove the forgeries from the bag. His light played over both sets of paintings; the frames matched perfectly.

Alfie used his flashlight to examine what fastened the pictures to the wall and found exactly what he had expected. He needed only a small wrench and a paring knife to remove them from the wall and set them on the floor.

He beckoned Eddie to watch him work, and thus, to learn something. He slowly removed the screws from each frame, and set the pictures against the wall.

Then the thing Alfie had expected least happened; the lights came on in the room.

"Stand very still," a man's voice said, "or I'll shoot you where you stand. Turn and face me."

The two men turned around and found themselves confronted by a large naked man, who was pointing a small pistol at them.

46

Alfie shrank inside his coat, making himself as small as possible. He knew the man with the gun would pay more attention to Eddie, the larger burglar. Alfie coughed a couple of times, holding his hands over his mouth, turning the man's focus to him, then away. He put his hands into his pockets and felt the cosh and the air gun.

The man with the gun stepped forward, put out a hand and spun Eddie around, a policelike move, as if he were going to cuff him. Alfie, seizing the moment of distraction, swung the cosh and struck the naked man in the back of the neck. He collapsed in a heap on the floor. Alfie put away the cosh and took out the air gun, previously reserved for a dog. It would work as well on a man.

Eddie turned, drew back a leg, and aimed a kick at the unconscious man's head.

"No!" Alfie said, but the leg was already swinging. Alfie put out his own leg and tripped Eddie, who fell backward onto the floor. Unfortunately, in so doing, he inadvertently pulled the trigger on the dart gun and shot the projectile into his own calf. He must have caught a vein, Alfie thought, because he felt a sudden rush that clouded his mind. Then he, too, collapsed, on top of the naked man.

Eddie got to his feet. "Alfie? It's Eddie. Are you all right?" Alfie was out.

Eddie turned his friend on his back and felt for a pulse. Slow and steady. He tried to be cool, now, as Alfie would have been. He knelt beside the paintings, put each of the forgeries into a frame, and fastened them to the wall again, then he tucked the originals into his bag and tidied up, putting the cosh, the tool kit, and the air gun into his coat pockets. He tried to find the dart, but couldn't.

Eddie was strong and Alfie was thin and light. He got his friend to his feet and over his shoulder, in a fireman's carry, then he picked up the bag containing the paintings and walked out of the study and down the hall to the kitchen door. He didn't bother relocking it behind him.

Eddie hurried down the steps and walked to the place where they had climbed over the wall. He set down his bag, hoisted Alfie to a position facedown on the top of the wall, then picked up the bag and scrambled up and over. From the other side, he got Alfie back on his shoulders, picked up the bag, and walked back to the waiting car. He found the keys in Alfie's pocket, then laid him on the back seat, stripped off his own raincoat and made a pillow for his friend, then he put the paintings in the boot.

A moment later he was behind the wheel, sweating freely, and starting the car. At the first roundabout he turned the wrong way, traveled 360 degrees around, and finally, came out on the correct road. He thanked God he had not met any traffic. All he had to do now was follow the signs to the motorway and stay on the wrong side of the road.

Felicity woke and found Stone gone. She couldn't hear him in the bathroom, so she put on a robe and went downstairs, where light was coming from the library door. Stone was lying on his belly, stark naked and, apparently, asleep. What the hell?

She kissed him on the shoulder and got no response. She pinched him on the ass, hard, and still, no response. She got him turned onto his back and felt his neck for a pulse: strong and steady. He coughed, and his eyelids fluttered.

"Stone, wake up," Felicity commanded, pinching his cheeks.

"Not now," he muttered. She slapped him smartly across the face. This time he responded, getting himself up on one elbow. "What the hell?"

"That's my question exactly," she said. "What are you doing downstairs and naked in the library?" Then she spotted the gun next to a chair leg. She helped him to his feet and into the chair. She thought of offering him a brandy, but decided that was not the thing to do; she wanted him awake, not drunk. She picked up the pistol, then expertly popped the magazine, racked the slide, and put down the hammer. "There, now you can't shoot me."

"Why would I want to shoot you?" Stone asked, rubbing his eyes.

"Why would you come downstairs, naked and armed?"

He thought about that and failed to come up with an answer. Dino walked into the library clad in a guest-room dressing gown, and saw Stone naked. "Jesus, Stone, you've got a perfectly good bed upstairs. What are you doing here?"

"He was out like a light when I came in. This was lying nearby," Felicity said, handing Dino the reassembled weapon.

"Who were you planning to shoot?" Dino asked him, dropping the pistol into the pocket of his dressing gown.

"He must have heard someone in the house," Felicity said.

"I must have heard something," Stone repeated tonelessly. He made a face and put a hand behind his head.

Felicity took the hand away and looked at his neck. "He's been coshed," she said.

"Is that some kind of a sex thing?" Dino asked.

"It's a club," she said. "He's been clubbed into unconsciousness."

"You want a drink, Stone?" Dino asked.

"That's not what he needs," Felicity said. "Can you walk, Stone?"

"Of course I can walk," Stone said, rising from the chair, then falling back into it.

"Let's get him upstairs," Dino said. He and Felicity each took an arm, got him to his feet, and marched him to the elevator. Upstairs, they got him into bed.

"I'll take care of him," Felicity said.

"I don't doubt it," Dino replied.

"You go back to bed, Dino."

"Yes, ma'am," Dino replied, then left the room.

Felicity went into Stone's bathroom, found a hand towel and got some ice from the machine in the bar. She wrapped up a handful of ice, then went back to the bed and tucked it under Stone's head. "That should make it feel better by the morning," she said.

She slipped out of her dressing gown and found the button that turned off all the lights, then got into bed.

Eddie made it back to Belgrave Square with no problems, parked the car, then got Alfie upstairs and onto his bed.

His wife got out of bed in her nightgown. "What's happened?" she asked. "Has Alfie had a stroke?"

"No," Eddie replied, "he accidentally received an injection intended for a dog."

"What dog?"

"There wasn't one. Just let him sleep it off." He helped her get Alfie's clothes off and found the dart in his leg.

He pulled it out and held it up. "He shot himself with this." Eddie went back to the car and removed the bag with the pictures and his raincoat from the car, put them in Alfie's study, then went back upstairs to bed. Nice payday coming, he reminded himself, as he drifted off.

47

Stone opened his eyes and put a hand to the back of his neck. It was wet, and there was a towel there. He looked at Felicity's side of the bed and found it empty.

She swept into the room from her bath, naked, and opened the curtains, filling the room with sunlight. "How are you feeling?" she asked, sitting down beside him and taking the towel from him.

"My neck hurts," he said, sitting up and turning his head back and forth slowly.

"You were coshed," she said.

"What?"

"Struck with a club or a blackjack. Apparently you heard something in the night, got a gun, and went downstairs. You probably disturbed one or more burglars at work and got coshed by one of them. I couldn't find another mark on your body. Dino and I got you to bed, and I put an ice pack behind your neck."

"Ah," Stone said, as if he understood, but he didn't. "The last thing I remember is you on top of me."

"What a sweet thought," she said, smoothing his hair.

"I can't remember anything else."

"It will come back to you in pieces," she said. "That's the way of these things."

There was a knock at the door; Felicity got into her dressing gown and pulled the covers over Stone. "Coming!" She allowed the breakfast cart to be pushed into the room, then dismissed the butler, and she and Stone had breakfast.

"I want to see what's missing from downstairs," Stone said, when they were done.

Felicity got him a dressing gown and went downstairs with him.

He looked around the room.

"Anything missing or awry?" she asked.

"Not that I can see." He sank into a chair.

"Are you feeling all right?" she asked.

"I think so," he said, rubbing his neck again.

"Let me know if you feel nauseated," she said. "That often happens after a blow to the head."

Stone got up and walked over to where his mother's paintings were hung and inspected them closely. "I think they're in the wrong order," he said, "but I'm still a little groggy."

Felicity looked at the pictures. "They look the same to me," she said. "Are you sure?"

"No," Stone replied.

"I think you could do with a bit more bed rest," she said, and led him back upstairs and tucked him in. "There," she said, kissing him on the forehead. "Sleep. I'll wake you for lunch."

Alfie came downstairs and joined Eddie for lunch. The ladies were shopping.

"How are you feeling?" Eddie asked.

"Much better," Alfie said. He leaned close to Eddie. "You could have killed him, you know. When you kick a man who's unconscious in the head, he has no defenses, can't see it coming. He can't even tense up to take the blow. You could have very easily broken his neck."

"I'm sorry," Eddie said

"You also made me shoot myself in the leg."

Eddie shrugged. "All my fault."

"What did you do after I passed out?"

"I put the fakes in the frames and reattached them, then I tidied up, hoisted you on my shoulder, took the bag and tools, and got out of there."

"Was the naked man still out?"

"Completely. I didn't mess with him. I got you back to the car and drove us home."

"In that case, we're lucky to be alive."

"Don't worry, I was careful to stay on the wrong side of the road."

"You mean, the left side of the road."

"Oh, yeah. What do we do now?"

"We get paid, and you go back to the States."

"I may still be hot there."

"You said they didn't even have a charge against you."

Eddie told him the story of his court appearance.

"They won't bother with you again," Alfie said, confidently. "As you say, they don't have a charge, except the one you've already pled to, and the judge has suspended your sentence. The courts are too busy to mess with those things. You're a free man."

"How do we get paid?" Eddie asked.

"I've phoned my man. His bloke will arrive here at two o'clock, and we'll be paid."

"In cash?"

"That's how it's done, my son, unless you'd rather have a check."

"I mean, I brought a couple of hundred grand with me and declared it to customs. I didn't know how long I'd be here. I can't haul all that cash into the States."

"Do you have a bank account on this side of the pond?" Alfie asked.

"No."

"I'd suggest Switzerland."

"I thought that was all over. No secret accounts anymore."

"I know a small private bank. It won't be a secret account, but nobody's going to ask them, are they? You can take a train to Zurich."

"I thought I might buy a car and drive around the continent for a few days."

"Good idea; I know a fellow who can get you what you want, and for export, all the right paperwork. You just have to pay the shipping, then the customs duty at the other end, when it arrives in the USA."

"Sounds good."

"What car do you want?"

"I was thinking a Mercedes, the big one."

"The S550?"

"Right."

"You want to pick it up in London or Zurich?"

"London."

They finished their lunch, and Alfie made a call, then handed Eddie the phone. "This is my mate Tom. Tell him exactly what you want," he said.

Eddie took the phone and had a discussion about color and options, then hung up. "He'll call me back."

Alfie looked at his watch. "My man's man should be here shortly. It would be better if you took a stroll around the square."

"Right," Eddie said. "If Tom calls back, give him my cell number."

"As you wish." Alfie settled into his chair.

Eddie went downstairs and took a stroll around Belgrave Square, then he stopped at a pub and had a pint of bitter.

Alfie took the paintings out of the carryall and looked them over. "Smashing," he said aloud to himself.

48

Eddie got back to Alfie's flat and found him in his study, looking very pleased with himself.

"Everything all right?" Eddie asked.

"Couldn't be better," he said, pointing to two identical aluminum cases. "Pick one. They've both got half a million pounds in them." Eddie picked one up and set it on Alfie's desk. It was very heavy.

"The combination for the locks is 3030," Alfie said.

Eddie spun the numbers into place and released the snaplocks. He opened the case and was greeted with stacks of twenty- and fifty-pound banknotes. He riffled through a few stacks to be sure there was no newspaper, just money, then he snapped the lid shut. "Thank you so much, Alfie," he said.

"You earned your half, Eddie. When things went wrong, you closed the deal and got us home safely." His telephone rang. "Yes? Hello, Tom. Come right up." He hung up and set his own case behind the desk. "I believe that's your new car being delivered," he said. "Put your case in the dining room, and go in there when you count out the cash. We don't want Tom seeing that."

Eddie picked up the case and carried it into the dining room, closing the door behind him.

There was a bustle at the front door, and a tall man in a tweed suit and trilby hat walked in with Eddie's and Alfie's wives, who were carrying lots of shopping bags.

"Oh, Eddie," Shelley said, "the new car is gorgeous. Tom showed it to us!"

"Ladies," Alfie said. "Will you excuse us for a few minutes while we transact some business?"

The women went upstairs with their loot, and Alfie introduced Tom and Eddie. Tom handed Eddie a file. "Here's all your paperwork," he said. "Certificate of origin, bill of sale, British registration—good for a year—U.S. emissions certification, driver's handbook, the window sticker listing all the options, and some photos of the car."

Eddie looked through them. "Looks good to me."

"If Tom says it's good, it's good," Alfie said.

Tom handed Eddie a bill. "All told, £143,051, including a year's comprehensive insurance," he said. "We'll call it £143,000 even, shall we?"

"Good," Eddie said. "Excuse me for a moment, I'll get your money from the safe." He went into the dining room, opened the case and counted out the money, then went back to the study. "Here you are," he said, "all in fifty-pound notes."

Tom examined the money carefully, and Alfie removed a large, buff envelope from a desk drawer and put the money into it.

They shook hands and Tom provided two sets of keys. "Would you like me to give you a tour of the controls?"

"I'll manage," Eddie said. They shook hands, and Tom left.

"Well, that was slick," Eddie said.

"Tom's a peach." Alfie handed him a ferry schedule. "I'd suggest you get up very early tomorrow and take the seven AM Chunnel train. It's about a two-hour drive down there. You should phone down and make a reservation."

Eddie did all that, and when the ladies came down for drinks, he told Shelley they'd be leaving the house at four AM.

"It's about 650 miles to Zurich," Alfie said. "I shouldn't think you'd want to stop for the night, given your cargo. Just go straight to the bank." He handed Eddie the bank's managing director's card. "I've already spoken to him. He'll wait for your arrival. Call him when you're an hour out. I'll book a hotel suite for you."

After dinner, Eddie loaded the car with the aluminum case and their luggage, then locked the trunk. The car was perfect. The following morning at four AM, they drove out of the garage. The traffic was very light, and they made excellent time. They checked in at the Chunnel an hour early and read the papers and drank coffee until boarding. By noon they were halfway to Zurich.

Eddie tried a couple of times to call Alfie to thank him again, but there was no reply. He switched his phone off the rest of the time.

Eddie phoned the banker, Karl Wirtz, an hour out, and continued to Zurich. Guided by the GPS they reached the bank. Eddie asked Shelley to wait, and he got the aluminum case from the trunk and rang the front bell. A man in some sort of uniform admitted him to the bank and took him up in the elevator to the top floor. The door opened directly into a foyer, and a small man in a good suit admitted him to an elegant office.

"Mr. Craft, I'm so relieved to see you," Wirtz said, showing him to a chair. "I've prepared all your documents for opening an account." He handed Eddie a file folder. "Please peruse them and sign where indicated. In the meantime, our accounting department will count your cash and give you a deposit receipt." The uniform took the case and left the room.

Eddie looked over the paperwork and signed where indicated. He looked at Wirtz, who still looked worried. "Why were you relieved to see me, Mr. Wirtz? You were expecting me, after all."

Wirtz's face fell. "I take it you are not aware of the events in London this morning?"

"No, we've been on the road since the wee hours."

"Then you will not know about Mr. Bing."

"Know what?"

"I'm very sorry to have to tell you this, Mr. Craft, but

we have been informed by our London office that Mr. Bing and his wife were shot and killed in their home this morning, while having breakfast. Their apartment was ransacked."

Eddie thought about that. They would have been through the Chunnel by that time.

A man came into the room and handed Eddie a document.

"Your deposit receipt, sir."

Wirtz handed Eddie a small document case, bound in alligator leather. "Here are your checkbooks, a debit/ATM card, which you must sign, your PIN number, and a bankbook, indicating your balance. You may write checks in any currency, anywhere in the world and the bank will automatically give you the best exchange rates upon receipt."

Eddie accepted the document case, but his mind was spinning. "Do you have any other details of Mr. Bing's death?"

Wirtz shrugged. "I'm afraid not. But Mr. Bing has been known, at times, to deal with people who are, shall we say, unorthodox. It is my supposition that you and Mr. Bing have had business?"

"Yes, we have."

"Have you booked a hotel room in Zurich?"

"Yes, Mr. Bing booked it for us."

"Then I would advise that you not keep the reservation, don't cancel, just ignore it." He took a notepad and wrote down a name and address. "This is a small, private hotel owned by a friend of ours, in the western suburbs of the city. I will book you a room there. Tomorrow, you should leave Switzerland. Paris is nice this time of year, I believe."

Eddie shook his hand and was escorted from the building by the uniformed man. He handed Shelley the address of their new hotel.

"Please enter this in the GPS."

"We're changing hotels?"

"I'll explain it to you later."

The GPS came to life and began issuing instructions. Eddie followed them to their new hotel. He parked, and a doorman dealt with the luggage. Once in their suite, he sat Shelley down and told her what had happened.

Shelley took it like a champ, Eddie thought.

"Are we in any danger, Eddie?" she asked.

"No one in the world knows where we are," he said, "except our new banker, who made the reservation for us. When we leave here tomorrow morning, even he won't know where we're headed."

"All right," Shelley said. "If you're not worried, I'm not worried."

49

Stone sat down to dinner with Felicity and the Bac-chettis.

"How are you feeling?" Viv asked.

"Normal," Stone said, "and I've remembered some-thing: two names, Alfie and Eddie. They were spoken when I was out, or nearly so."

"Spoken by whom?" Felicity asked.

"A man's voice. British, I think."

"Eddie is probably the guy the feds are looking for," Dino said.

"What's his last name?"

"Craft." He turned to Felicity. "He's somebody who may know something about a crime in the States."

"I can have him looked up," Felicity said. "Excuse me for a moment." She left the room.

"That's not much to go on," Stone said.

"You came here expecting a burglar," Dino said, "and one found you. You were also looking for a burglar named Eddie. Sounds like a good lead to me."

Felicity returned and took her seat. "Mr. and Mrs. Craft arrived the day before yesterday," she said, "and immediately went to ground. They're not registered at any hotel in the U.K."

"That was my information," Stone said.

"We've also taken note—in the dim past—of a burglar named Alfie Bernstein," she said. "He disappeared nearly twenty years ago after completing a prison sentence."

"If he disappeared, he would have changed his name," Viv said.

"No doubt, but we've no idea of that name," Felicity said. Her phone rang. "I'll just take this here, if that's all right," she said. "Yes?" she listened carefully, then hung up. "A new Mercedes was registered yesterday to an Edward Craft, at an address in Belgrave Square," she said. "The leaseholder's name is Alfred Bing, who has no record with the police or anybody else, except . . ."

"Except what?" Stone asked.

"Except that Mr. Bing and Mrs. Bing were murdered in that same flat this morning, while breakfasting."

Stone blinked. "And where were Mr. and Mrs. Craft at the time of the murder?"

"They left the country on the seven AM Chunnel this morning," Felicity said. "So, they're somewhere in Europe in their new Mercedes. I've noted the registration number."

"Then they must have left London very early this morning—certainly no later than five-thirty," Stone said.

"Just so," Felicity replied. "They are not suspects in the deaths of the Bings."

Dinner arrived, and they gave it their attention. When they were on coffee, Stone said, "I should phone in this information to the FBI." His turn to leave the room. He called Maren Gustav and filled her in.

"I'm impressed," she said. "How would you like to become an FBI special agent?"

"Less than almost anything in the world," Stone replied. "If you'll excuse me, I still have dinner guests to attend to." He hung up and returned to the library.

Felicity was on the phone again, listening intently. Finally, she hung up. "My people have had a word with the New Scotland Yard," she said. "The Bing flat in Belgrave Square was stuffed with objets d'art and paintings. More than a dozen pieces and pictures have been identified as stolen—and that's just for a start. They have another forty or so to check out."

Stone stared at his mother's four pictures on the wall. "I mentioned this before, but now I'm sure. Those pictures are in a different order than they were when we got here."

"Yes," Felicity said, "you did mention that, but you had recently been rendered unconscious, so I dismissed the thought."

"Let me get some tools," Stone said, and left the room with a sinking feeling in his heart. He was already thinking about how to recover those pictures.

At that moment, Eddie and Shelley were dining at the Hôtel Ritz, in Paris. They were occupants of a handsome suite, and their new Mercedes was tucked away in the hotel's garage.

"Eddie," Shelley said. "Aren't we a little exposed here?"

"No, because I checked in under the name of Charles Gwynne. I happened to have a spare passport in that name. So do you, but I haven't given it to you yet. You're Claire Gwynne. We'll have to get you a wedding ring tomorrow. We'll need to lift a license plate from a similar Mercedes, as well."

Stone unfastened the fourth picture and set it on the floor beside the others. He freed one from its frame and examined it closely, then he turned it over and inspected the back of the painting. He set that down and inspected the other three in the same way. "I must say, I thought I had this figured out, but I don't."

"Explain, please," Felicity said.

"Well, I was—due to circumstances beyond my control—alone in a room for some time with two professional thieves, who had, presumably, come here to steal something. And yet, I can't demonstrate that they stole *anything*. I thought they had, perhaps, replaced my mother's paintings with copies, but all four of these are genuine. Believe me, I know my mother's work." He fastened the paintings to the wall, this time in the correct order, then joined the others for cognac.

"Well," Dino said, "your thieves must have already begun their work, when you arrived on the scene, because they put the pictures back on the wall in the wrong order."

"I suppose that must be so," Stone admitted.

"You discovered them at their work," Viv said, "and that must have discombobulated them considerably. I mean, the sudden appearance of a naked man with a gun would rattle anybody."

Felicity clapped her hands. "They were so discombobulated, they put the originals back and left with the forgeries!"

"What forgeries?" Viv asked.

"The ones they intended would replace Stone's mother's works. Stone, do you remember anything you saw when you entered the room? Think about it."

Stone closed his eyes and tried to imagine himself entering the library. Finally, he spoke. "The pictures were not on the wall," he said. "There was just a blank space! Then the lights went out."

"The pictures were probably on the floor," Felicity said. "They had to put something on the wall, or you would have known the next morning that all four had been stolen. But in their rattled state, they put back the originals and left the premises with the forgeries!"

"That seems highly improbable," Stone said.

"Then think of another scenario," Felicity said. She waited for a moment. "Anyone? Anything at all?"

"Felicity is right," Dino said. "What is Occam's razor?"

"The simplest solution is usually the correct one," Viv said. "If you hear hoofbeats, think horses, not zebras."

"And in this case, Felicity's solution is not just the simplest solution, it's the *only* one," Dino said.

"Also," Stone said, feeling enlightened, "it solves two crimes. This one and the murder of Alfred Bing and his wife."

"How so?" Felicity asked.

"Bing must have had an order for the paintings—a dishonest collector, no doubt, since they couldn't have been sold publicly. So, the client paid for the paintings, then had them checked out and discovered they were forgeries. Then he went back to Bing's flat—or, more likely, dispatched someone else—with orders to get back his money. The police said the flat had been ransacked, so maybe he got it back. Then the dispatched guy dispatched the Bings!"

"I love it!" Felicity said, laughing.

"But," Dino interjected, "if he got his money back, he only got half of it, because Bing must have already paid off Eddie Craft. I mean, he bought a very expensive car, then left the country in the dead of night."

Everybody laughed, then they had another cognac.

50

And then, a few hours after their flight from Paris, the rains came to Miami. "Let's get out of here," Eddie said to Shelley.

"I miss home, in New York," she said. "You think we'll be okay on the airlines?"

"I'm not taking that chance," he said. He called the concierge and had them booked in a drawing room on a train that evening.

Maren, reunited with Stone in New York, rolled over and woke him.

"Mmmph," Stone said.

She fondled him. "Any interest?"

"Always," Stone replied, turning to her.

Over breakfast, Maren took a call, then hung up. "Eddie Craft was spotted landing in Miami yesterday," she said. "We're canvassing hotels there."

"You should canvass flights to New York, too."

"It's being done."

Stone munched thoughtfully on a sausage. "How about trains?"

"A train?" she asked. "You can still get a train to New York from Miami?"

"I think so, but I'm not sure. I'd check, if I were you."

Maren got on the phone and spoke for five minutes. "There is such a thing as a train, and all the reservation lists are being checked." An hour later, she got a call.

"Thank you." She hung up. "He's not on anybody's reservation list."

"What if he's traveling under another name?" Stone asked.

"You're a big help. Got a name for me?"

"I don't."

"Then shut up, please."

Stone thought it a good time to take a shower.

Early that evening Eddie and Shelley got off the train at Grand Central and were met by a porter, who took them to a waiting town car. "Do you think somebody might be waiting for us at your place?" Shelley asked.

"Let's see." Eddie called the doorman's station in his building. "This is Mr. Craft," he said.

"Good evening, Mr. Craft," the man replied. "Are you on your way home? There've been some gentlemen waiting, asking for you."

"No, Walter, I'm stuck in London for another couple

of weeks," Eddie said. "Be sure and tell that to anybody who asks." He hung up. "Is your place still available?" he asked Shelley.

"Sure. My girl comes in once a week and cleans." She gave the driver the address, three blocks from his apartment house.

It was small, but attractive and comfortable, Eddie thought. He settled into a reclining chair and switched on the TV. He had missed TV while in Europe; all they had was CNN, no Fox News.

Stone was watching MSNBC, while Maren was packing. He heard her phone ring, then she hung up and came into the bedroom.

"Eddie Craft is back in New York," she said.

"One of your people spotted him?"

"Not exactly."

"Ah, wiretap."

"Don't say that word. Somebody might be listening."

"Nevertheless."

"We're not using it to gather evidence," she said, "just to gather Eddie. He called his doorman to ask if anyone had asked about him. That means he's thinking about going home."

"I thought you said he was home already."

"In the city. Not at home in his apartment."

"You can tell that with a wiretap?"

"I didn't hear that, and I won't answer it."

"Okay, where in Manhattan is he?"

"Within a six-block radius of his apartment house."

"In what direction?"

"Northeast."

"Then all you have to do is a little basic navigation."

"Navigation?"

"Let's say you're on a boat, and you want to find your position."

"Okay, let's say that."

"There's a lighthouse on the chart you're using to navigate. Let's say the lighthouse is Eddie's apartment building."

"Okay."

"You look at your compass, then at the lighthouse. Let's say it's at 210 degrees; that means it's southwest of you. Now, on your chart you draw a line from the lighthouse at 030 degrees, which is the opposite of 210 degrees. Your position is somewhere on that line."

"Got it. Where on that line?"

"To learn that you need a second landmark. Let's say there's a mountain peak to the right of the lighthouse. You draw a line from the mountain peak, until it crosses your first line. Where they cross is your position. So, you see, one landmark gives you direction; the second gives you distance."

"There are no mountains in Manhattan," she said. "What do I use for the second landmark?"

"How about the gate to Central Park at Sixty-sixth Street?" Stone got out a city map and drew the two lines for her. He pointed to where they crossed. "Eddie is in this building right here, probably a townhouse with sev-

eral apartments in it, since that's mostly what you have
on that block."

"Which floor is Eddie on?"

"For that, you have to use a different navigational
technique."

"What is that?"

"You ring the bell."

"Which bell?"

"All of them, and you have men positioned on each
floor, so when Eddie emerges, they introduce themselves
with their badges, then arrest him on a material witness
warrant. You do have such a warrant, don't you?"

"We do."

"Well, there you are. Go get him!"

Maren picked up her phone and gave the person who
answered the address. "Eddie Craft is in that building,"
she said. "Station men on each floor, then ring all the
bells. When he comes out, take him into custody and
take him to the office." She hung up. "That was bril-
liant," she said.

"Any Sea Scout could do it," he said. "Perhaps the
FBI should recruit from the Sea Scouts."

"Good idea."

Eddie was trying to digest the latest conspiracy theory
on Fox when the doorbell rang. As he rose to answer it,
he heard the bell upstairs ring, then another above that.
He went to the peephole and peeped into the hallway. At
the right edge of his view, the brim of a hat could be

seen. Eddie sensed immediately that the hat rested on the head of an FBI agent.

Eddie hurried into the kitchen, where Shelley was scrambling eggs, and raised the window beside her and looked out. A fire escape beckoned. "Listen," he said. "Wait until I'm out the window, then go to the door with a spatula in your hand and play dumb. And put this on." He handed her an apron, then stepped through the window, closed it behind him, then walked down one flight.

Shelley put on the apron, picked up the spatula, and, impulsively, picked up the small skillet in her other hand. She opened the door. "Yes?" she said to the man lurking there.

"Eddie Craft?" he said.

"Really? I look like an Eddie?"

"Is Eddie Craft here?"

"Who is Eddie Craft?"

"He lives here."

"Not in this apartment," she said.

"Do you know in which apartment?"

"I've lived here for six years, and I never heard of him," she said. "Try another building."

"What are you cooking, there?" the agent asked.

"Scrambled eggs. Want some?"

"No, thanks, it just looks like a lot of scrambled eggs for one person."

"I'm hungry," she said. "Make up your mind."

"Good day to you," he said, touching the brim of his hat.

"And to you," she said. She turned and kicked the door shut, then went back to the kitchen, set down the eggs, and opened the window. "Eddie," she called. "The eggs are ready, and the coast is clear."

"Coming," Eddie called back.

51

Washington, D.C., police chief Deborah Myers sat at her desk, reading the file of one Edward Craft, who had become her obsession, and who continued to elude her. The telephone rang and she absently answered it. "Chief Myers."

"Chief," a male voice said.

Before he could say another word, she stopped him. "I know who you are. What do you know?"

"I know that the person is back in New York."

"Where?"

"The Bureau located him by some sort of GPS thing, on his cell phone. Write this down."

Debby grabbed a pencil. "Go."

He gave her an address on East Sixty-sixth Street. "The Bureau got a search warrant and went through the whole building, but the only thing they turned up was a woman he used to know, named Shelley Moss. They found her alone in her apartment, cooking breakfast. She was cooperative but denied any current knowledge of him. The agent had a good look around and found nothing to indicate that he had been there."

"I'll be at the Lowell," she said, then hung up and buzzed her secretary.

"Yes, ma'am?"

"Get hold of Rocco Turko, and tell him to grab his ready bag and meet me downstairs. Order my car and the King Air to Teterboro, and have a car and driver meet me there, at Jet Aviation, and to stick with me for a week."

"Is that how long you'll be gone?"

"Depends. Refer any important calls to my cell phone, but you call me on my second cell phone, to keep things confidential. Got it?"

"Got it, ma'am."

Debby grabbed her ready bag and makeup kit from her office closet and ran for the elevator. Rocco Turko was standing in the building's garage when she got there. He was a tallish, handsome, squarely built man of forty who, in his double-breasted overcoat, resembled a refrigerator. "Morning, Deb," he said. He was one of only a few colleagues who was allowed to address her informally.

"Have you still got that NYPD badge?" Rocco had done ten or so years with the NYPD and, when he left, had "forgotten" to turn in his badge.

"Yep."

"Good, you may need it." They got into the car.

"Why are we going to New York?" Rocco asked.

"Eddie Craft," she replied.

Rocco didn't have to ask why. He knew that Craft was

the only witness who could testify that she had been in the police evidence locker on the date that some things disappeared from that place.

"Is he coming back with us?" Rocco asked.

Debby gave him a look that he interpreted as a firm "No."

She reached into her ready bag and withdrew a black .22 semiautomatic pistol, with a silencer screwed into the barrel. "It has a loaded magazine. It's all you'll need."

Rocco accepted the weapon, unscrewed the silencer, and put it and the pistol into separate pockets. If he had needed a further answer from his chief, he had it.

In the late afternoon, Maren came back to Stone's house and found him in his study.

"Hi, there," he said, rising and giving her a kiss.

"Hi. How's your jet lag?"

"Okay, but I still have a sore neck."

She reached to massage his neck, but he flinched. "I know a chiropractor who makes house calls," she said.

Stone sat next to her on the sofa. "Call him for me, will you?"

Maren reached for her phone. "Her," she said. She made the call and hung up. "She'll be here in half an hour. She says it's okay for you to have a drink before she gets here."

"Is that her prescription or yours?" Stone asked, standing and going to the drinks cabinet and returning with a Knob Creek for him and a Laphroaig for her.

"Both," Maren said.

They tapped glasses and drank. Stone resisted reaching for anything else: too little time.

Joan came into the study. "Your manipulator is here," she said. Stone laughed.

"Are you ready to be manipulated?"

"I am ready."

A small, pretty woman came in, pushing a folded table on wheels and introduced herself as Pru Hawkins. They shook hands. She asked him to remove his shirt and lie facedown, and he did so.

"I can see where it hurts," she said. "Feel it, too." She asked him to turn over, then lifted his head and turned it slowly back and forth. "Did the bourbon help?" she asked. "I can smell it on your breath."

"It did," Stone said.

She turned his head to one side. "Take a deep breath and let it out slowly."

He did so, and she made a quick movement that caused a noise in his neck. She repeated the movement with his head turned the other way, and got the same sound. "Now, sit up," she said.

Stone sat up and turned his head back and forth. "Much better," he said. "You freed it up. It's still a little sore, though."

"I prescribe another bourbon for that," she said. She folded up her table, set it on its wheels, named a number, Stone paid it. Then she was gone, leaving her card.

———

Eddie got out of a cab in front of the Colony Club, a womens' association that occupied a chunk of Park Avenue, next door to his apartment building. It was raining steadily, and even though he was already wearing a trench coat and a fedora, put up a golf-sized umbrella, shielding him from the view of an unhappy-looking man on the street corner, who had a view of his apartment building's front door.

Eddie walked through the Colony's entrance, into an empty lobby, which sported much paneling and marble. His heels echoed as he walked quickly through a door next to the unocupied front desk, past the men's room in a hallway. He walked farther down the hall and into a scullery, off the kitchen. A solitary man was scrubbing pots and paid him no heed. Eddie took a right turn, opened a larger door, and emerged into the alley between the club and his building, where deliveries were made. It was raining even harder than before, and he put up his umbrella again.

He walked a few yards to a corner and peeked around it, toward Sixty-third Street. The alley rose to a wrought-iron gate, and through its bars he saw another man, dressed much the same as the one on Park, and looking just as unhappy. His back was turned, so Eddie continued to watch him, until he turned and walked toward the entrance of the apartment building. Eddie took that opportunity to run to his building's alley entrance, past the gymnasium and the laundry room, to the service elevator. He pressed the 14 button and the elevator rose to that floor and disgorged him at the kitchen entrance to his apartment.

He furled his umbrella, stepped to a dry spot nearer the door and took off his shoes, then he unlocked the door and let himself quietly into his kitchen.

52

Eddie walked carefully to the door to the dining room, which also acted as his study. He opened the swinging door a couple of inches and listened. Nothing.

He entered the dining room, which gave him a wide view of his living room, and checked for any differences—cameras, microphones, things moved. Still nothing. He checked both bedrooms and baths and could find nothing that indicated visitors, except for the maid, then he hung his wet coat in the hall closet and stuck the umbrella in a stand by the front door.

Finally, he went into his study, opened the bottom drawer of the little chest next to his reclining chair and removed a throwaway cell phone. He cut away the packaging with scissors and found it forty percent charged. Then he called Shelley's apartment.

"Yes?"

"Are you alone?"

"Yes."

"Good. Come be alone with me. It's raining like hell, so take an umbrella and use it to shield your face from the two guys watching the building. Don't walk, get a cab."

"See you as soon as I can get a cab," she said.

He hung up, and the housephone rang. "Yes?"

"Welcome home, sir," the doorman said. "Just checking to be sure you were the one in the elevator."

"I was, Terry," he said. "But I'm expecting company. She'll be in a cab, so greet her with your umbrella, and make it tough on our two visitors outside."

"Will do, sir."

Eddie hung up, poured himself a Scotch, sat down in his recliner, plugged in the throwaway to recharge and switched on the TV. The weatherman said it was raining and would continue to do so throughout the day.

The King Air had to fly an instrument approach, something that always set Debby's teeth on edge, but the runway appeared in the aircraft's windshield right where it was supposed to, and they landed safely.

Her usual driver was waiting on the tarmac with an umbrella and helped them into the car, then put away their luggage. He dropped them at the Lowell, where Debby went to her suite and Rocco went to his usual single, reserved for the help.

Less than a block away, Eddie received a dripping Shelley and her bags and gave her a kiss. "Did they spot you?"

"Sure, but they couldn't see my face—or anything else, come to that, what with the rain and the umbrellas."

She got settled, then poured herself a drink and sat in his lap.

"Home again," she said. "Are we prisoners here?"

"We can come and go, but by a circuitous route. I'll show you the way."

Debby called her FBI mole on his throwaway. "Yes?"

"I'm here; where is the guy?"

"We haven't seen him. The old girlfriend left her apartment in the cab, but our people lost her. It's rotten outside."

"All I want is fifteen minutes alone with him."

"You'll get it when we find him. I can't do any better than that."

"I pay you too much," she said, then hung up.

Stone was dozing in bed when Maren's phone rang and she answered it. "What a coincidence!" she said, then hung up.

"What's a coincidence?" Stone muttered.

"Both Eddie Craft and Little Debby are in the same city—this one."

"Where?"

"She's at the Lowell, he's in the wind. My people had a chat with a former girlfriend of his but had no indication that they are in touch."

"Hang on to her," Stone said. "She's all you've got."

"We haven't got," Maren replied. "She left her building in a cab, in this pouring rain, and they lost her."

"If she doesn't come home tonight, she's with Eddie," Stone said. "Probably in a hotel."

"We're already checking the hotels," she said.

"It will be a very good one, because Eddie is now rich."

"According to customs, he was carrying twelve thousand dollars when he landed in Miami," she said, "and he declared it. Where's the rest of it?"

"Where's his new Mercedes?"

"I don't know. You think the money is in the trunk?"

"Not unless he's a bigger fool than I think he is," Stone said. "I think he's found a banker."

"In London?"

"Scotland Yard would probably know about it. Switzerland, maybe. Or Malta, that's more secure."

"You make everything seem so complicated," Maren said.

"Life is complicated. If it were simple, we wouldn't need an FBI."

53

Rocco Turko left Debby's suite with his instructions. It would be a dry run, but he would do it properly and go as far as he could.

He removed a zippered case from his luggage and surveyed his choices: two moustaches, one Vandyke, and one full beard. He chose the beard and glued it firmly into place, using the bathroom mirror.

He dressed in gray trousers, a white shirt, and a blue blazer. Then he put on his reversible raincoat with the tan side out and chose a foldable Trilby hat, with a plaid tweed cap for backup, tucked into a pocket with his glasses. He put on thin leather gloves, then picked up the silenced .22, disassembled it, wiped the gun, the magazine, and the cartridges very clean. Then he reassembled it all and tucked it into an inside-the-belt holster, with the barrel and silencer protruding but covered by his trousers.

A quick look of approval in the mirror, and he left the room, went downstairs, and exited the hotel via the service door. He opened his umbrella and used it to partially conceal himself from the view of the waiting FBI men down the block. He passed the wrought-iron gate to the alley and noted that it had no keyhole; which meant electric operation. Then, as he approached the apartment building, he got lucky. A black town car turned onto East Sixty-third Street and pulled up before the building's awning. Rocco brushed past one of the FBI agents, whose gaze was fixed on the arriving car. The doorman came outside with a big umbrella and began assisting an elderly woman and her luggage from the vehicle.

Rocco turned right behind the assemblage and walked into the building's lobby. He stopped at the doorman's desk and looked at his list of occupants. An Edward Craft was there, in 14D. A sign hung on a hook over the desk, reading TERRY ON DUTY. The service elevator, he remembered, was through one door and down a short hallway. The car stood there, its door open. He boarded it and pressed fourteen.

The door opened into the service hallway; he looked to his left and saw a door marked C, then to his right and saw another, marked D. He readied himself, unholstered the weapon, pulled down his hat brim a bit, and rang the bell.

A moment later a man's voice said, "Who is it?"

"It's Terry, Mr. Craft," Rocco replied. "From downstairs."

He heard the lock slide and saw the door open an inch. He put his shoulder into it and knocked Eddie

Craft backward onto the marble floor. Craft managed to get to his hands and knees, and Rocco struck him firmly with the weapon on the back of the neck. Craft collapsed into a heap. He would be out, Rocco reckoned, for at least twenty minutes, perhaps half an hour.

He walked across the kitchen and through an open door into a dining room, apparently also used as a study. There was a large reclining chair before a window. Rocco stepped up onto the chair, unfastened the lock, raised the window and stuck his head out far enough to see the ground. The alley below was empty.

Rocco went back to the kitchen, hauled the still-unconscious Craft to his feet, and slung him over his shoulder. He walked into the dining room, perched Craft on the back of the recliner, then took him by the ankles and tipped him backward and out the window. A couple of seconds, and Rocco heard the *thud* from below. He had another look out the window, and found the alley still empty, except for the bleeding heap that was Eddie Craft. He put the pistol back into its holster and moved back toward the kitchen door, then he stopped in his tracks. A sleepy-looking woman in a nightgown was standing in the living room near what Rocco assumed was a door leading to the bedroom.

"I was asleep," she said, sounding drugged.

"It's all right," Rocco replied. "Go back to sleep." He turned her around gently and guided her into a bedroom, then tucked her in.

She rolled onto her left side, with her back to him.

Rocco thought about it for a moment: what he had

here, he said to himself, was a very convenient murder-suicide. He unsheathed the pistol, stepped over to her, and put a bullet through her right temple. The small-caliber slug didn't make a mess, just a neat hole. He shot her once more in the back of the head, then left the room and went back to the dining room. He looked out the window and saw Craft, still undisturbed. He held the gun out the window and dropped it. It bounced off Craft's body and lay near him.

Rocco had a look around the dining room and kitchen for traces of his visit and found none. He retrieved his umbrella, left by the kitchen door, and pressed B in the elevator. It descended with no stops. His luck was holding.

In the basement, Rocco had a look around and saw a woman on a treadmill in the gym, her back to him. He walked past the laundry to the side door of the building and found a box to the right of it labeled GATE. He pressed the button and looked outside. The wrought-iron gate was slowly swinging open.

He walked quickly to the top of the alley and checked the street. The two FBI agents were standing under the awning at the entrance, earnestly engaged in conversation.

The gate began to close itself, and Rocco stepped through the gap, opened his umbrella, and put on his heavy, black-rimmed glasses, folded and pocketed the Trilby and put on the tweed cap, then he turned and walked toward the agents, who ignored him as he passed. He walked to the corner of Park Avenue and turned south, then right on East Sixty-fourth. The streets were mostly empty because of the rain.

Shortly, he was at the hotel's service entrance and took the elevator upstairs. Back in his room, he stripped off his clothes and put them into a plastic bag marked *dry cleaning*. He filled out the ticket and put that into the bag, too, then hung it on the doorknob. Then he went into the bathroom and used a solvent to free the beard, which he washed and dried with the hair dryer, then put back into its case. Finally, he showered, scrubbing with a brush the areas that had been exposed.

He dried his hair with the hair dryer, got back into his robe, found his slippers and his key card, then walked down the hall to Debby's suite and knocked softly on the door.

"Who's there?" she asked from inside.

"Rocco."

She opened the door, still dressed in her robe, and closed it behind him.

"Tell me how it went," she said.

"From all appearances, Mr. Craft had a disagreement with his girlfriend, and he shot her twice in the head as she lay in bed. Then he went into his study, opened a window, and departed for the alley below. He was still in the alley, undisturbed, when I last saw him. I dropped the weapon after him, and it rests near his body. Then I got the hell out of there."

"Rocco," she said, kissing him and feeling for the opening of his robe, "you're a wonder."

"I believe I am, at that," Rocco replied, freeing her of her garment.

She led him to bed. "Let's celebrate," she said, pulling him in behind her.

"Hip, hip, hooray!" Rocco said.

54

Stone and Maren were taking a walk up Park Avenue in the late afternoon when Maren got a call. She stopped. "Excuse me for a moment, Stone. Yes?" She listened intently. "What's the address? Cross street? I'll be there in ten minutes." She hung up and took Stone's arm again, and they walked on. She was very quiet.

"Is anything wrong?" he asked.

"Well," she said. "It appears that I've lost my witness, who could have convicted Little Debby."

"Eddie Craft?"

She nodded. "We're only a few blocks away. You're an old homicide detective, Stone. I'd like you to give me your take on this." She wouldn't say more.

They reached East Sixty-third Street and crossed Park. "Here we are," she said.

"This is Dino's building."

"I know." They entered the building, and she flashed her badge to the doorman.

An agent stood nearby. "I'll take you up, Director," he said, then led the way to the elevator.

The door to apartment 14D stood open, and Stone could see men down the hall in the living room.

"This way," their agent said, pointing at the doorway. "Bedroom is right, then left."

Stone and Maren bent over the body. "One in the temple, one in the back of the head," he said. He saw a pill bottle and read the label. "Ambien."

"This way, Director," the agent behind them said. He led them through the living room to the dining room, where a window stood wide open. "Stand on the chair and look down," he said, then helped Maren up. She got down, and Stone took a turn.

"Any conclusions?" Maren asked Stone.

"Only the obvious ones: he shot her twice while she was sleeping, then took a dive out the window, taking the gun with him. It's next to the body. I'd like to hear from the medical examiner before I go any further."

"Why would he shoot her?" Maren asked.

"The ME isn't going to tell us that. My guess is they were married or longtime companions, and that makes this a case of domestic violence. They're unpredictable before the fact and, often, unsolvable afterward, unless you can locate a few good friends and hear what they have to say about the relationship. My guess is that Eddie was a loner, except for his girl, so he wouldn't have a lot of friends."

"You don't see anything professional in this, then?" she asked.

Stone shook his head. "Not unless your crime scene team comes up with some DNA or other evidence indicating the presence of a third party."

"So, it's a murder-suicide?"

"Probably. It would be a hard thing for a pro to plan, but he might have done it on the fly, found himself in circumstances that required killing them both. Someone recently mentioned Occam's razor to me."

"We'd never solve anything, if we didn't look beyond Occam's razor," she said.

"Good point, but why tie yourself in knots? If you hear hoofbeats, think horses, not zebras."

Maren managed a chuckle.

"I think you would spend your time more profitably looking for someone who can back up Eddie's story about Little Debby stealing the gun from the D.C. evidence locker."

"We've already interviewed his neighbors in the lockup. The cop in charge was in the john with a crossword."

"Hang on," Stone said.

"What?"

"Let's go take a look at the scene in the alley."

They rode the elevator down and walked outside, then around the corner. The rain had stopped an hour before, but they had to avoid puddles.

Eddie's body was a crumpled heap, and the weapon lay nearby. "What kind of weapon was stolen from the evidence room?" Stone asked.

"A .22 semiautomatic pistol with a silencer," Maren said.

Stone pointed at the gun near the body. "Voilà," he said.

They were walking back up the alley when the ME's van backed in. Maren slapped a palm on the fender; it stopped and a door opened. She gave the man her card. "Call me when you're done; I don't want to wait for the written report."

They walked on up the alley to the street. "Let's steal a car," she said, pointing at an FBI vehicle.

"Go right ahead, Director," an agent said.

"Hello, Karl. I'd like you to get a ballistics report on the weapon at the scene. It resembles one stolen from a D.C. evidence room, and I want a comparison."

"Yes, ma'am," the man said. They got into the car, and Maren gave the driver Stone's address.

They were at dinner that evening, at Patroon, with the Bacchettis.

"I don't like people getting killed in my building," Dino said. "Or jumping out windows. It's bad for property values."

Maren's phone rang, and everybody kept quiet while she listened. Finally, she hung up.

"What?" Stone asked.

"The gun in the evidence room was used in a homicide, so they had a full ballistics report on it. They did another at our offices on the gun found near Eddie's body. It's the same weapon."

"No doubt?" Stone asked.

"No doubt."

"What does that tell us?" Maren said.

Stone sighed. "I'm trying to think of a scenario that would make possible the use of this gun in two murders, in separate cities."

"One murder," Dino said.

"Two," Stone replied. "The woman was shot twice." Dino nodded.

"Can you think of such a scenario?" Stone asked.

Dino squinted. "Little Debby steals a gun from the evidence room in D.C., then she gives it to the guy who's about to testify against her, so he can use it on his girl-friend before he offs himself?"

"You see the problem," Stone said to everybody. "I can't make it make sense."

Maren shook her head. "It happened, so there is a scenario. We just have to figure it out."

"I need another drink," Stone said.

55

Stone and Maren were getting into bed, but sex was not on either of their minds.

Stone froze for a moment, deep in thought.

"There was a third party in the apartment," he said.

Maren turned and stared at him. "Why do you think that?"

"Because it's the only thing that makes any sense. Debby stole the gun from evidence, not Eddie, right?"

"That's true."

"And Eddie hotfooted it out of the country to England, as soon as he hit the street. He may even have been the guy who coshed me."

"'Cosh' is an old-time criminal's word," Maren said. "Eddie's friend, Alfie, probably coshed you."

"My point is, Eddie was in the room; he was in the country in England. He was not someplace where Little Debby could hand him the gun. In fact, she probably stole it to use it on Eddie. Wait a minute, wasn't Donald Clark shot with such a weapon?"

"I believe he was."

"Okay, compare the ballistics of the gun in custody to that of the Clark bullets."

Maren tapped out an e-mail and sent it. "We should have that tomorrow, since the record already exists for both shootings. Now, what else?"

"Do we believe that Little Debby shot Clark and Eddie herself?"

"I don't. She had an ironclad alibi for the Clark murder. My bet is she'll have one for Eddie's death, too."

"You read the ME's report," Stone said. "Were there any bullets in Eddie's body?"

"No, they're saying the fall killed him."

"Where's the report?"

She went to her handbag, produced it, and gave it to Stone. "Okay," Stone said. "'Death resulted from head injuries resulting from a fall from a fourteenth-story window.' There's no mention of a slug in the body." He read on. "Wait a minute, there were some marks on the body not associated with the fall."

"I didn't get that far," Maren admitted. "I probably would have later. What were the marks?"

"An elongated bruise on the back of the neck," Stone read, "and another mark, but not a bruise, over the right kidney. I remember the body lying on its left side," Stone said. "Leaving it open to the injury above the kidney."

"Go on; the rest of the scenario, please."

"I'm not a doctor, but let me play one for a minute."

"Go right ahead, Doctor."

"A bruise is formed by blood collecting under the skin

from an injury, breaking tiny blood vessels, I think the little blood vessels are called capillaries."

"Right."

"So, our third party hit Eddie across the back of his neck, rendering him unconscious, but not dead, so there was still blood flowing to collect under the skin, forming the bruise."

"Agreed."

"The other injury, the one over the kidney, did not form a bruise, so we can posit—I love that word, *posit*—that Eddie was already dead when he suffered the non-bruising blow above the kidney."

"One injury before death, one after," Maren agreed. "I buy the gun being used for the blow to the back of the neck, but what caused the one above the kidney?"

"The gun," Stone said.

"But it didn't cause a bruise."

"Here's how it went, to my mind," Stone said. "First of all, I was wrong about the guy not being a pro. He was very much a pro. He gets into the apartment—probably Eddie let him in—he slugs Eddie, who goes out like a light. Then he opens a window and tosses Eddie out."

"Why do you think that?" Maren asked.

"Because Eddie went out the window—no question about that. And if he was unconscious at the time, it was because the third party in the apartment—the pro—made him that way."

"I buy that," she said. "Tell me about the girl."

"The pro would have cleaned up after himself, so he's looking around, and he finds the girl in bed, asleep—

she's taken Ambien—and he finds it necessary to improvise, so he shoots her. But he has to hang the murder on Eddie, so he goes back to the open window and tosses the gun out. Eddie is lying, dead, in the alley, and the falling gun strikes him over the right kidney, then bounces off to where your agents found it. I'll give you odds there are no fingerprints on the weapon, because Eddie couldn't make any, and the pro would have wiped the gun, because he couldn't put Eddie's prints on it at that time, and he certainly didn't want his own on the weapon."

Maren took herself through the scenario, making little gestures as she thought, then stopped and looked at Stone. "I buy it," she said, "all of it. Horses, not zebras. Now I'm too excited to sleep."

"Let me make another suggestion," Stone said, reaching for her.

56

They slept quietly through the night, sated with each other. The bell on the dumbwaiter woke Stone at seven. They finished their sausage and eggs quietly and were having coffee when Stone spoke.

"We've got another problem," he said.

"Swell," she said, "and just when I thought we'd—or rather, you'd—worked it out. What is the problem?"

"We don't know who the third party was—the pro."

"Oh, shit."

"And how are we going to find out?" he asked.

"Well," Maren said, "pros don't take out an ad in the *Times*, do they?"

"They used to do that in *Soldier of Fortune* magazine," Stone said, "but I'm not sure that's even still in business."

"I haven't heard of it in years," Maren said.

"How well do you know Little Debby?" he asked.

"I've had a drink with her. I think we've been at the

same dinner party a couple of times, but I can't say I *know* her."

"Who's her best friend?"

"Donald Clark," she replied, "but she apparently got tired of him."

"Do you know of anybody who knows her well?"

"She's not the sort to have a lot of friends, and certainly not the kind she would confide in about how to hire a pro."

They finished their coffee and went to their respective showers.

Debby awoke in a bed that was empty on the other side, but still a little warm. She called Rocco's room.

"Yes?"

"Aren't you coming to me for breakfast?"

"I didn't think I should be there, naked, when the room service waiter arrives."

"Well, there is that."

"You order, I'll shower and dress. Call me when the waiter has gone."

"I'll do that." They both hung up.

They had breakfast at the table in Debby's sitting room. "Is it too early for us to scram?" she asked.

"Do you want to stick around until the cops call on you?"

"Why should they do that?" she asked.

"Well, if the only person who could give credible testimony against you takes a dive out a high window, they might have a few questions for you."

She looked at her watch. "I'll give them until we're ready to check out, then we're out of here. Call the driver for me, will you? Here in an hour?"

"Certainly," Rocco replied.

At his desk later in the morning, Stone called Dino.

"Bacchetti."

"Let me run a scenario by you about Eddie Craft's death," Stone said.

"You know that's a federal matter, don't you? Craft had already been served with a subpoena."

"Well, yeah, but listen to this anyway. I just want to know if you think it plays."

"Okay, I'm listening."

Stone took him through his theory of the murders, pausing frequently to answer Dino's questions. Finally, he was done. "What do you think?"

"I think you've crafted a theory to match the circumstances, but that doesn't mean it will convince a jury. You've gotta come up with the third guy, the pro."

"And even if we do, why is the pro going to tell us all?"

"Tell you what. You find the pro, then leave him in a room with me for half an hour, and he'll tell *me* all."

"So your plan is to beat it out of him?"

"Of course not! You know we don't do that anymore!"

"I do?"

"Trust me, you do."

"Okay, okay, but if we're going to find the pro, we're going to have to get his name out of Little Debby, and if we left her alone in a room with you for half an hour, *she'd* probably beat *you* up."

"You wound me," Dino said, sounding wounded.

"No, but Little Debby certainly would."

"Whatever," Dino said.

"So, who do you know who knows what makes Little Debby tick?"

"Donald Clark," Dino said, "but he's out of action."

"You're a big help. Anybody else?"

"Maybe," Dino said.

"Don't be coy. If you've got something, spit it out."

"Okay," Dino said. "How's this for a trail of bread-crumbs for you to follow . . . Little Debby had a rep for liking her lovers in pairs, didn't she?"

"Yes, and sometimes treys."

"Then ask somebody she fucked."

"Well, let's see: I can think of three, and two of them are dead. In fact, it has just occurred to me that one of them, Deana Carlyle, died the same way Donald Clark did."

"Deana Carlyle? Producing another victim isn't going to get you the name of the pro, but she was somebody's girlfriend, wasn't she?"

Stone snapped his fingers. "That's it!"

"Did you snap your fingers?" Dino asked. "You hardly

ever do that. You must have come up with something good."

"Art Jacoby," Stone said. "Deana was his girlfriend, and they've both been in the sack with Debby."

"And Art hates her, so he knows her well!"

"Is he sitting down the hall from you?"

"Hang." Dino put him on hold. "Nope," he said finally, "he called in sick. He should be home in bed."

"Thank you, pal." Stone hung up and called Art. The call went straight to voicemail. "Art, it's Stone. Call me, please." He tried the landline: busy, busy, busy.

Maren walked into Stone's office, looking fresh. "Good morning again," she said.

"I found somebody who knows Little Debby well," Stone replied. He called Art again, got the same trip to voicemail.

"Come on," he said, standing up and getting into his jacket. "We're going to go see him."

"See who?"

"Art Jacoby," Stone said. "He's a detective on the DCPD."

"Why does he know Debby so well?"

"Because they hate each other."

"What better reason?" she asked. "Let's go."

57

It had begun to rain again, this time with lightning and thunder. The car was being hammered. They arrived at Art Jacoby's place, and, in the lobby, were stopped by a man behind a desk.

Stone flashed his honorary gold shield.

"Sorry, but the guy upstairs has one of those, too, and he gave strict orders that no one is to come up."

Maren pulled out her badge and pointed to the line on her ID that read DIRECTOR. "This trumps them both," she said, "or would you feel better with half a dozen angry special agents in your lobby?"

"All right," the main said. "I'll call upstairs."

"You won't get an answer," Stone said. "We're not sure he's still alive."

The man held the phone away from his ear. They could all hear the busy signal. He replaced the receiver. "Please, go right up," he said.

They went right up. Art's room was next to the elevator, so they didn't have a long walk. Stone rapped on the door. "Art," Stone called out, "open up. It's Stone Barrington." No response. This time he hammered on the door with his fist and shouted, "Open up!"

"Listen," Maren whispered.

Stone leaned over to hear her better. "What?"

There was a loud explosion and a large hole appeared in the apartment's door, exactly where Stone's face had been, sprinkling them with bits of wood and dried paint.

Stone pushed Maren back and shouted from a couple of feet away. "Art, it's Stone Barrington! Stop shooting at me."

"Stone?" a voice called from inside. "Is that you?"

"Yes, it's me. Stop shooting at us."

"Who's 'us'?" Art asked suspiciously.

"Maren Gustav. Does that name ring a bell?"

"From the FBI?"

"How many Maren Gustavs do you know?"

"Come in," Art called back. "It's unlocked."

Stone turned the knob and pushed the door, then stood back. "Put down the shotgun," he called.

"It's down. Come in."

Stone indicated to Maren that she should enter. "You first," she said.

"I'm coming in," Stone said, then stepped through the door.

Art Jacoby was standing on a sofa across the room, a police-issue riot gun at port arms. "Don't worry, I'm not going to shoot you," he said.

"Then come down off that sofa and stop looking so threatening!" Stone shouted. "I've had about as much of this as I can take before I start shooting back!"

"All right, all right," Art said, placatingly. "I won't shoot."

"Does that include me?" Maren asked from the doorway.

"Jesus, it's you," Art said, stepping down off the sofa.

"Who were you expecting?" she asked.

"Debby Myers," he replied, as if she should have known all the time.

They sat at Art's little kitchen table and drank terrible coffee that he had just brewed. "Good to the last drop," he said, licking his chops.

Stone rolled his eyes. "No Italian would ever drink this," Stone said. "Have you ever met an Italian?"

"I've put a few in prison," Art said, "but we never had coffee together."

"Can we get down to business?" Maren asked.

"What business do we have?" Art asked.

"The business that made you shoot through the door, because you thought Little Debby was out there."

"Oh, *that* business. What do you want?"

"First," Maren said. "Why do you think Debby wants to kill you?"

"Well," he said, "she killed my girlfriend. She killed Donald Clark. She killed Eddie Craft, Frank Capriani, and Patricia Clark. Why should she make an exception for me?"

"Art," Stone said. "Why do you think Debby killed Eddie Craft?"

"Well, he's dead, isn't he? After all, he was going to testify against her about the gun she stole from the property room. She wouldn't need a better reason than that."

"You think she did all these murders herself?"

"Of course not. She isn't stupid."

"Then who did she get to kill them?"

"My best guess is Rocco Turko," Art said.

Stone looked at him blankly. "Who the hell is Rocco Turko?"

"Think Rudolph Valentino, with a little more weight and a few more years. In short, Little Debby's type."

"She has a type?"

"Well, she's fairly liberal about that, I guess. Let's just say he's the ideal: good-looking, well-hung, and willing to do anything she wants, in bed or out."

"Including killing people?"

"Oh, that's his favorite thing," Art said. "At DCPD, he holds the record for apparently unprovoked shootings. If he walked in here now, he'd be happy to put two in both your heads, if that's what Little Debby wanted. Frankly, I was expecting *him*. That's why there's a hole in my door. Incidentally, I'm very sorry about that. I've been drinking a lot of coffee to stay awake for when he showed up, so I'm a little wired."

"A little," Stone said.

Maren spoke up. "Where can we find this Rocco Turko?"

Art shrugged. "Find Debby, he'll be there. She never travels without him, he's her official security detail and her unofficial supply of cock."

"Do you know where she is right now?" Maren asked.

"In New York, I imagine. That's where Eddie Craft and his girl were when they found him."

"Any idea where?"

"She always stays at the Lowell, Sixty-third and Madison."

"Then that's where we should be," Maren said, standing up and getting out her phone. "I need a SWAT team at the Lowell Hotel, at East Sixty-third, just east of Madison. We're looking for Deborah Myers, chief of the DCPD, and, especially, a DCPD police officer named Rocco Turko, whom you may expect to be armed and extremely dangerous. And—this is very important—I'll be there in fifteen. Don't start without me."

"Can I come along?" Art asked. "I'll bring my shotgun."

"Sure, Art," Stone said. "You'd better reload."

58

They arrived a few steps away from the Lowell, and as they got out of Stone's car, he spotted a large, unmarked, black van at the opposite curb, idling, making its contribution to global warming. "That's us," Maren said. She raised a small radio to her lips.

"Willie, what's up inside?"

"Chief Myers just called for a bellman, so I think they'll be right down."

"I'm going in. Don't send in the boys unless you hear gunfire."

"Yes, ma'am."

"Let's go," Maren said to Stone and Art. "And, Art, hang your raincoat over your arm to conceal the shotgun. No shooting, anybody, unless one of them starts it."

Stone nodded and followed Maren into the lobby of the hotel. A bellman walked past them, pushing a cart of luggage, headed for the curb. Stone looked up at the elevator lights and saw one on the way down. "Descending," he said to Maren.

"Got it," she said. She centered herself on the elevator and stood there loosely, her hands folded in front of her.

The elevator opened and Deborah Myers stepped into the lobby, followed by a man who looked like Rudolph Valentino, but older and heavier and a sex addict, from what she had heard.

"Why, Maren," Debby said, making an effort to smile. "What a surprise! What brings you to the big city?"

"I was hoping to run into you, Deborah," Maren replied, "and my luck is good today."

"What can I do for you?"

"I'm so glad you asked. I wondered if you and your bodyguard could take a ride with me downtown?"

"For what purpose?" Debby asked.

"There are some questions I'd like to ask you, and I hope you'll have some answers."

"The hotel has a conference room. Why don't we go in there?"

"I'm afraid the nature of my questions requires a more official setting."

Debby thought about it for a couple of seconds, then smiled again. "Sure, be glad to. I assume you have a car?"

"A very comfortable one," Maren replied and headed with Debby for the street. "Stone," Maren said over her shoulder, "would you give a lift to Deborah's security man?"

"Of course," Stone said, showing Rocco the Bentley, with Fred braced at the open door. "Art, will you ride shotgun?"

Art smiled. "Sure, Stone."

No one in either car spoke on the ride downtown.

At the federal building, everyone placed his weapons in a tray and passed through the metal detector. It took Rocco three passes, to unload two handguns and an evil-looking knife.

Upstairs, Debby and Rocco were escorted to different interrogation rooms. Maren waved for Stone to follow her to an office, where she rang for a secretary, then dictated two documents, while Stone waited outside. When she was done, Maren motioned him inside and closed the door. She took off her jacket and began to unbutton her silk blouse.

"Really?" Stone asked, surprised. "In an FBI field office?"

"No, not really," Maren replied. She took off the blouse, reached behind her and unhooked her bra, revealing what Stone had always felt was one of the finest views on the planet.

"You're pressing your luck," Stone said.

"Be a good boy, and you can watch me with Rocco." Stone's jaw dropped.

She put on the blouse again, but left the two top buttons undone, then she picked up a file folder from the secretary and started out of the office. Maren pointed at a door in the hallway. "You can watch from in there," she said.

An FBI special agent came out of the interrogation room, bearing all three of Rocco Turko's weapons, and Maren stepped in.

Stone took a seat and looked at Rocco, sitting calmly at the table in the interrogation room. He could hear him clear his throat.

Maren entered the room, and to Stone's surprise, Rocco stood up to greet her.

"Good morning, Mr. Turko," Maren said, offering her hand.

"Good morning," he replied, shaking it.

"May I call you Rocco?"

"Of course."

"And you may call me Maren," she said. She took off her jacket and in so doing, her breasts nearly, but not quite, escaped her blouse. "I'm so glad we could get together."

"So am I," Rocco replied, smiling to reveal some very fine dental work.

"Listen, I know you're going to want a lawyer, but if you can hold off that request for a few minutes, I don't think you'll need one."

"Fine with me," Rocco replied.

"First of all, are you acquainted with two people called Eddie Craft and Shelley Moss?"

"I don't believe I am," Rocco replied.

"Never met them?"

"No, not that I can recall."

"Would you recognize them if you saw them?"

Rocco shook his head. "No."

"They live in an apartment building at East Sixty-third Street and Park Avenue . . ."

Rocco began shaking his head.

". . . in apartment 15D," she said.

Rocco froze. "Say again?"

"Park and Sixty-third, apartment 15D."

Rocco seemed unable to speak.

"Perhaps you know the people who live one floor below them, in 14D—a Mr. and Mrs. Moskowitz."

Rocco's mouth opened, but no sound came out.

"Mr. and Mrs. Moskowitz"—she consulted a sheet of paper in her hand—"Leo and Mandy—were involved in a very unfortunate incident yesterday—an apparent murder-suicide. Leo shot Mandy, then exited his apartment through an open window, falling to the alley below. No one we've questioned can understand it. They seemed such a happy couple."

"I didn't know them," Rocco finally managed to say.

"Obviously not," Maren said. "You will recall that yesterday was a very rainy day."

"I recall that."

"Did you notice that some water had collected on the floor of the service elevator?"

Rocco began to shake his head, then stopped. "What service elevator? At the hotel, you mean?"

Maren smiled. "No, Rocco." She leaned forward just a little, to give him a better view of her cleavage. After that, Rocco didn't look anywhere else.

Maren picked up the phone on the table and said, "Bring them to me, please."

An agent walked into the room and placed a handsome pair of shoes, complete with shoe trees, on the table. "These are very nice," Maren said.

"Not mine," he said.

"Oddly, we took them from your luggage and"—she pulled out the tree from one shoe—"they were made by a gentleman called Sylvano Lattanzi, in Milano, Italy."

"If you say so."

She held up a shoe. "And here's a nice little label in the shoe that says 'Made expressly for Rocco Turko.'"

"Oh, well . . ."

"Oh, well, indeed, Rocco." She opened the folder next to her on the table and took out a photograph and held it up beside the shoe.

Rocco tore his eyes from her cleavage long enough to look at the photograph and the shoe.

"You will note that the heel on your shoe is identical to the heel mark in the photograph, which was taken in the kitchen of apartment 14D."

Rocco's jaw was working, and he was licking his lips.

"You know what that means, Rocco. You're a cop, after all, and I'll bet you've investigated hundreds of murders and the evidence that they turn up, like this photograph. It means that you were in apartment 14D, yesterday."

"I think I'm going to need to speak to an attorney," Rocco said. "Right now."

"Give me a couple minutes more, Rocco, and I don't

think you'll need one, because I'm going to make you an offer you can't refuse, as the Don said in *The Godfather*." She leaned even further forward.

"We've got you dead to rights on the murders of the couple in 14D," Maren said. "So what you're looking at, Rocco, is the rest of your life in a maximum-security federal prison, where you're in your cell, alone, for twenty-three hours a day."

Maren deftly undid one more button, just to be sure she had his undivided attention. She did. "It also means that, for the remainder of your days, you will never again have sex with a woman."

Rocco made an involuntary whimpering noise.

"But Rocco," Maren said, regaining his attention, "it doesn't have to be that way. Would you like to hear how it could be?"

"Yes," Rocco said, hoarsely.

"If you tell me everything you know about the murders of Donald Clark, Deana Carlyle, Eddie Craft, Shelley Moss, Patricia Clark, and Frank Capriani—Eddie Craft and his girlfriend lived in apartment 14D . . . sorry, my mistake about that . . . then you can plead to the murders in 14D, and I have already taken it upon myself to speak to the U.S. attorney for the Southern District of New York, who has agreed to recommend a sentence of seven to ten years, out in five, and not in a maximum-security facility, but in a Club Fed in Florida, where the winters are kind."

Rocco sat back in his chair and took a couple of deep breaths.

"It's a limited, onetime offer, Rocco, and it expires in thirty seconds. What's it going to be?"

"I agree," Rocco replied. "I'll take the plea."

"A wise decision," Maren said, taking a document from her file and handing it to Rocco with a pen. "You will note that I have included in this agreement the fact that you committed these six murders on the instructions of Deborah Myers."

"Fuck her," Rocco said, then signed the agreement.

The secretary entered the room and handed Maren a longer document.

"And this," Maren said, handing it to Rocco, "which is a transcript of our conversation today. Ms. Banks, here, will witness both documents."

Rocco signed, then he looked back at Maren's cleavage. "I want to see them," he said.

"I'm sorry, Rocco," Maren replied, "but that sort of thing will have to wait for five years."

Two agents came into the room, handcuffed Rocco, and took him away.

Stone walked out into the hallway, and when Maren emerged, he followed her back to her office, where she stripped off her jacket and blouse and got back into her bra.

"Well," Stone said, "I've had a better day than Rocco. And that was an interrogation technique entirely new to me."

She laughed and gave him a kiss.

Then they heard a ruckus outside in the hallway, and

Stone recognized the voice of Little Debby, who was screaming oaths about Rocco Turko. He opened the door and watched her being dragged past by two female agents.

"There was a speaker in the room where she was waiting," Maren said. "She heard every word that Rocco spoke."

END
Washington, Connecticut
May 2, 2020

TURN THE PAGE FOR AN EXCERPT

While settling in for some downtime in New York City, Stone Barrington suddenly draws the attention of an anonymous enemy. This nameless foe's threats hit close to home, and before Stone can retaliate, the fearsome messages turn into very real consequences. With the help of old friends—and a lovely new tech-savvy acquaintance—Stone sets out to unravel the fatal agenda. But as the web of adversaries expands, Stone realizes that no place is safe, and he'll have to flush out the mastermind before he and those closest to him are silenced for good . . .

1

Stone Barrington awoke slowly on a Sunday morning. The evening before had been spent with his good friend Dino Bacchetti, and had involved good beef, good wine, and various spirits before and after dinner. Stone was alone in his bed, which was not his preference.

He was alone in his house, too, he recalled, since he had given his cook and housekeeper, Helene, and her husband, Fred Flicker, the weekend off. There was, he remembered, a housemaid stationed in the kitchen to meet his culinary needs. He picked up the phone and dialed an extension.

"Yes, sir?" an accented voice responded. "This is Gilia."

Gilia was Greek, being one of a number of Helene's nieces who occasionally landed in his employ.

"Breakfast," he said huskily.

"Your usual, sir?" she asked.

"Yes, thank you."

"Only a little minutes," she replied.

"Good." He hung up.

Gilia had been taught well. The eggs were soft and creamy and properly salted, the sausages were tender and juicy, and his Wolferman's English muffin was perfectly toasted and buttered. By the time he had wolfed it all down, he felt restored. He was searching for an old movie to watch on TV and had just selected a John Wayne western, John Ford's *Rio Grande*, when his cell phone rang—the secure one. He picked it up. "Speak," he said. It was likely to be one of two people on the line; he hoped it was the tender gender one.

"What kind of greeting is that?" she asked.

"A cautious one," Stone replied. "I was hoping it was you and not Lance." Lance Cabot was the director of Central Intelligence, for whom Stone served as a special adviser. The woman on the line was the President of the United States, Holly Barker, with whom Stone had had an affectionate relationship for many years, off and on.

"I was thinking of coming to New York," she said. "When would be convenient for you?"

"How about right this minute?"

"You understand there are arrangements to be made."

"I thought we had that all ironed out and given a code name, 'Turtle Bay.'" That was the name of the neighborhood surrounding a private garden on which his house was located. "All you have to do is dial a number, speak those words, and you'll be here in time for lunch."

"I know that's supposed to be how it works," she said, "but I've never actually used it. And things have a way of going awry when their operation depends on the workings of the federal government."

"Oh, ye of little faith," Stone said, reprovingly.

"My faith in my government, or lack of same, is based on long experience."

"But your experience at the top of it is brief," he replied. "Try it and see."

"Hang," she said, picking up another phone and dialing an extension. She held the other phone so he could hear the conversation.

"Yes, Madam President," a male voice said after a single ring.

"Execute Turtle Bay," she said.

"Your helicopter will arrive in thirty minutes," he replied. "ETA, East Side Heliport in one hour and forty-two minutes. Weather is favorable all the way. A three-car SUV group will greet and transport you to your destination."

"Excellent," she said, and hung up. "You get that?"

"I did. Sounds as if it should work as planned," he said. "Do you want to go out for dinner?"

"You know we can't appear in a New York restaurant without causing a press riot."

"Then I'll have you all to myself."

"You could invite the Bacchettis," she replied.

"Done."

"I'll look forward to that. Tell Viv I'm dressing to kill. See you soon."

Stone looked forward to it as well. He called another number.

"Bacchetti," a gruff voice replied.

"Which one?"

"The one who didn't have to go through menopause."

"Holly's on her way. Dinner here this evening?"

"Viv will want to know what we're wearing."

"You and I are wearing tuxedos. Tell Viv to let her imagination run wild."

"I can't do that. It would mean an all-afternoon shopping trip and a big dent in her credit card."

"*C'est la guerre*, pal. Six-thirty for drinks." He hung up. Then, as he did, he remembered that Helene was away for the weekend, and he was *not* cooking in a tuxedo, or out of one, for that matter. He called Fred's cell phone.

"Yes, sir?"

"I'm sorry to disturb you, Fred," Stone said, "but our friend Holly is coming to dinner, as well as the Bacchettis, and I don't know if Gilia can handle that."

"One moment, sir." He came back a moment later. "Helene says Gilia can manage with what's in the fridge and the pantry. She'll call her with instructions. Not to worry."

"Thank you, Fred," Stone said and hung up, feeling relieved.

Holly arrived with four pieces of luggage and one Secret Service agent, a woman named Midge. The other agents had to loiter in the garage or around the neighborhood.

She flung herself into his arms. "I want you," she said, "but I need a nap."

"You know where the bed is," he said, leaving Midge to get Holly's luggage aboard the elevator. Stone looked in his study for a book he had been reading but didn't find it; so he went downstairs to his law office and did. He was about to leave the room when there was a trumpet fanfare, and a message appeared on his desktop computer screen. Stone walked over, sat down, and read it.

Dear Sir,

Your computer, its hard disk, and all your programs and files are now frozen. Please understand that I have been reading them for weeks and, as a result, I know everything there is to know about you—your address and phone numbers, your social security number, your tax returns, and all your financial information are at my fingertips. I can dump your stock portfolio and deposit the funds in any bank account, anywhere. I can publish your tax returns in your local newspaper. I can print and distribute all the deeply personal e-mails you have sent to women over the years, some of them well-known to the public. In short, I can make your life a permanent hell.

But I am a reasonable person, and I will provide you with a means of avoiding these disclosures. All you have to do is to purchase one million dollars'

worth of Bitcoin on the Internet and transfer them
to an account that I will provide details for later.
Upon receipt, your files will be restored, your
computer unlocked, and it will be as if you never
had the pleasure of meeting me. You have until
noon Friday next to accomplish this: if you should
fail to meet that deadline, your life will lie in ruins.

There is a window at the bottom of your screen
where you may send me an e-mail, should you
wish.

Regards,
Dodger

Stone read it again, then pressed the Print Screen button and waited for the printer to spit out the copy. When
it had done so, he typed GO FUCK YOURSELF into the
e-mail window. Then he took his book upstairs and settled in to read.

2

It was the best kind of dinner: old friends, a comfortable atmosphere with a cheerful fire burning in the grate, and a dinner that was nearly as good as Helene's would have been. Afterward, the ladies excused themselves for a trip to the powder room. They might as well have been in London, Stone thought.

"What's new?" Dino asked.

Stone took a folded sheet of paper from an inside pocket and handed it to him. "This is new," he said.

Dino read it, twice. "Are your computers blocked?"

"Mine is. I didn't try Joan's."

"Are you going to pay the million bucks?"

"Of course not!" Stone said, with as much restraint as he could muster.

"You're pretty hot about this, then," Dino said, leaning back in his chair and sipping his cognac.

"Wouldn't you be?"

"Me? I would have already turned this over to our tech guys and forgotten about it."

"I don't have a tech staff on call," Stone said.

"Don't you? There's Bob Cantor; there's that ki
Huey, that you worked with on the *New York Tim*
thing. And of course, there's Lance Cabot, who has t
tech world at his fingertips."

"Oh, them. Well, I guess I could call one of them."

"Call all of them," Dino advised. "Otherwise, you'
going to find yourself with thousands of dollars' wort
of useless computers. Oh, and then there's the scandal,
your attacker stumbles into your e-mails from Lance."

Stone took a big gulp of his cognac and swirled
around in his mouth before swallowing. "It's embarras
ing," he said.

"I think Lance is going to find it more than embarrass
ing," Dino said. "He's been sending us all those repor
from the field, along with the analyses."

Stone winced. "You're right. I'm going to have to ca
him."

"And then . . ." Dino said slowly, "there's Holly.
expect you have quite a few e-mails from her in an en
crypted file."

Stone sucked his teeth and bathed them in brandy
"Thank God they're encrypted," he said.

"Your computer was encrypted, too," Dino pointe
out. "And yet . . ."

The women returned in time to keep Stone from ex
ploding.

"What's wrong?" Holly asked Stone.

"Wrong? Not a thing."

"I'm not buying that."

"And look at Dino," Viv said. "He's just scored some big point. So Stone's ox has probably been gored."

"We're not talking," Dino said smugly.

"Stone?" Holly said.

"Dino's not talking."

"Dino," Viv said, "you're going to tell me."

"If I feel like it," Dino replied airily.

"You may want to reconsider your position."

"It's Stone's problem. He can tell you, if he wants."

"It's something I'd rather keep to myself," Stone said firmly. "For the moment."

Later, Holly crawled into bed with Stone and slung a leg over his. "Are you sure you don't want to tell me?"

"I'll handle it myself," Stone replied, giving her a long kiss.

"You're trying to distract me from the subject?" she said.

Stone kissed her again and threw in a caress to a place she loved. "Is it working?"

It was working.

Stone arrived at his desk the following morning, approximately on time, and his secretary, Joan, knocked and came in. "We don't have any computers," she said. "Just black screens. Nothing works. Shall I call somebody?"

Stone thought about that: if he said no, he'd never hear the end of it. He handed her the sheet of paper.

She read it carefully. "There's nothing pertaining to

you, explicitly. He doesn't use your name, address, or phone number. It's a scam. He sent out a zillion of these and it's just a phishing expedition. Don't bite."

Stone said nothing.

"You bit," she said firmly.

"I only told him to go fuck himself."

"Hook, line, and sinker," she said.

"Hardly that."

"Now he knows you exist. Before, you were just a file name among millions he stole from some mailing list. And it never hurts not to be disrespectful. What's in it for you to piss him off?"

"You're exaggerating the problem," Stone said. "From now on, I'll just ignore him."

His computer made a rude buzzing noise, and he and Joan both looked at the screen.

Now, it's a million and a half.

Stone swung around and aimed for the keyboard. Joan took hold of his chair and held him back. "Don't, you'll just make it worse!"

"How could it be worse?" Stone asked.

"Well, he could be listening to our conversation."

Stone opened his mouth to speak, and he clapped a hand over it.

"Shush."

Stone nodded and removed his hand.

Joan whispered in his ear, "Call Lance."

AUTHOR'S NOTE

I am happy to hear from readers, but you should know that if you write to me in care of my publisher, three to six months will pass before I receive your letter, and when it finally arrives it will be one among many, and I will not be able to reply.

However, if you have access to the Internet, you may visit my website at www.stuartwoods.com, where there is a button for sending me e-mail. So far, I have been able to reply to all my e-mail, and I will continue to try to do so.

If you send me an e-mail and do not receive a reply, it is probably because you are among an alarming number of people who have entered their e-mail address incorrectly in their mail software. I have many of my replies returned as undeliverable.

Remember: e-mail, reply; snail mail, no reply.

When you e-mail, please do not send attachments, as I never open these. They can take twenty minutes to download, and they often contain viruses.

Please do not place me on your mailing lists for funn stories, prayers, political causes, charitable fund-raisin petitions, or sentimental claptrap. I get enough of tha from people I already know. Generally speaking, when get e-mail addressed to a large number of people, I im mediately delete it without reading it.

Please do not send me your ideas for a book, as I hav a policy of writing only what I myself invent. If you sen me story ideas, I will immediately delete them withou reading them. If you have a good idea for a book, writ it yourself, but I will not be able to advise you on how t get it published. Buy a copy of *Writer's Market* at an bookstore; that will tell you how.

Anyone with a request concerning events or appear ances may e-mail it to me or send it to: Putnam Publicit Department, Penguin Random House LLC, 1745 Broad way, New York, NY 10019.

Those ambitious folk who wish to buy film, dramatic or television rights to my books should contact Matthev Snyder, Creative Artists Agency, 9830 Wilshire Boule vard, Beverly Hills, CA 98212-1825.

Those who wish to make offers for rights of a literary nature should contact Anne Sibbald, Janklow & Nesbit 285 Madison Avenue, 21st Floor, New York, NY 10017 (Note: This is not an invitation for you to send her you manuscript or to solicit her to be your agent.)

If you want to know if I will be signing books in you city, please visit my website, www.stuartwoods.com where the tour schedule will be published a month or sc in advance. If you wish me to do a book signing in your locality, ask your favorite bookseller to contact his Penguin representative or the Penguin publicity department with the request.

If you find typographical or editorial errors in my book and feel an irresistible urge to tell someone, please write to Sara Minnich at Penguin's address above. Do not e-mail your discoveries to me, as I will already have learned about them from others.

A list of my published works appears in the front of this book and on my website. All the novels are still in print in paperback and can be found at or ordered from any bookstore. If you wish to obtain hardcover copies of earlier novels or of the two nonfiction books, a good used-book store or one of the online bookstores can help you find them. Otherwise, you will have to go to a great many garage sales.

STUART
WOODS

"Addictive . . . Pick it up at your peril.
You can get hooked."
—*Lincoln Journal Star*